YOUNG BLOOD

A WITCH HUNTER SAGA NOVELLA

NICOLE R. TAYLOR

PART I

TWO YEARS AGO…

CHAPTER 1

Liz Evans was a mess.

Well, that's what she felt like every day since she'd graduated high school. The world told her she was meant to go to a great college, get a degree, and have a highflying career in...

That was the problem.

She had absolutely no idea and at twenty, she was still waiting tables at the local café where she'd worked her entire senior year. Yep, she was one of those people. The ones who got stuck and could never get out of whatever small town they grew up in.

That small town was Ashburton, Louisiana. Complete with its stifling humidity, dose of colourful eccentrics, rednecks, and thankfully, a large population of sane people to balance it out, it was her home. For the moment, anyway.

In high school, she'd been a blonde-haired, blue-eyed beauty. Popular enough, considering she had no ambitions to be on the cheerleading squad or student council. She'd had good grades and all the obvious extracurriculars on her flawless transcript... So why was she so clueless? It was a mystery she was still trying to work out, but in the meantime, she was working on getting into a collage, any college, and waiting for a big, fat welcome package to arrive in the mail.

She stood behind the counter at Mrs. Greene's Café and finished wiping down the coffee machine so it would be ready to be fired up tomorrow. The bell over the door jingled as a familiar sight walked in.

"Hey, Alex," she said, leaning against the counter.

Alex was one of her best friends—the other being Gabby Cohen—and wasn't interested in the big city college life one bit. Alex worked over in the botanical gardens as its chief landscaper and floral engineer, otherwise known as a gardener. The only gardener, which saw him exhausted most days.

Pulling out a takeout container from the warmer,

she handed it to her friend and smiled. "Scored you some leftover lasagna from lunch."

"Thanks, Liz." He sighed, leaning his large frame against the counter. "You're a lifesaver."

"As long as you're eating," she scolded. "You work too hard."

He was probably the most selfless person she'd ever met. In school, he'd been this tall, lanky, ginger-haired bully target, but now he was built, handsome, but still just as sweet.

"Yeah, yeah," he said with a chuckle. "The day I can get a partner to help me out is the day I ease off, you know that."

"You're too much, Alex."

Holding the takeout container to his chest, he gave her a wave. "Likewise."

Waving back as he left to go home, she resumed her cleaning duties, wondering if today was the day she'd go back to her apartment and find the letter that would change her life. She didn't have much time to think about it because the bell over the door burst to life again as Gabby jabbed it open and ran in, looking all wild and flustered.

"Liz?" she called out.

"Gabby, what's wrong? Did something—"

"I've got something to show you," she said, interrupting her friend. "Are you finished?"

"Yeah, but—"

"C'mon, before I lose my nerve." She grabbed her hand and tugged her toward the door.

"Whoa, Gabby. What's going on?"

Gabby was always a little flustered, but something was up today. For such a small town where nothing much happened, it had to be something big.

"I'll explain when we get there." She waved her other hand, dismissing her friend's questioning.

Liz had no choice but to call out to her boss as Gabby dragged her out the door. Whatever this was, it ought to be good.

Gabby Cohen was a witch. At least, that's what she figured when she started doing things that were impossible. But it wasn't until a chance discovery that she understood what was happening to her.

Her grams had left her a spell book—a grimoire —hidden in Gabby's parent's attic, concealed amongst the dusty boxes of her childhood toys. It was written in a strange language she couldn't decipher, but there were a few pages in English she could understand. Spells for sparking fire, incantations for levitation, rituals to help her sense out the Earth, and more.

She'd spent the last few months trying to figure it out on her own because if she told someone, they'd all think she was crazy.

She'd gone out to the old cemetery by the abandoned Degaud manor the night before and worked her biggest spell yet. At one end of the plot was a stone statue of an angel holding a child. It was worn and covered with splotchy yellow lichen and when she'd levitated the whole thing right off the ground, she knew this secret was too big to keep on her own.

If she was going to tell anyone, it would be Liz.

Liz was her best friend and one of the first people she'd met when she first moved to Ashburton in the seventh grade. She would understand. Well, she'd probably be the most accepting, considering the crazy things they'd gotten up to when they were younger.

She drove along a back road through the darkening forest in the beat-up hunk of metal she liked to call a car. Liz sat in the passenger seat, a look of total confusion on her face. Turning off into the long driveway that led to the cemetery, Gabby pulled the car onto the side near a pair of large, wrought iron gates. Nobody came here, not even a caretaker, so the entire place was spooky and overgrown, especially with the long shadows cast by the dipping sun.

"Um, Gabby?" Liz asked, looking through the windshield. "Why are we at the old cemetery?"

"It works better out here," she muttered, killing the engine.

"What works better? Gab, you're kinda freaking me out. If you're going to go all axe murderer on me, this is the perfect place."

Laughing, she gave her friend a wink. "As if."

Getting out of the car, they walked into the cemetery and weaved their way through the tombs and graves that dated back to before the days of the Civil War.

This whole area had been settled in the early 1700s by the French who came to build New Orleans, so there were family names like Perot, Rousseau, Degaud, and LaRoux etched in stone. All of them were families that'd been amongst the first to settle here. It was a shame that no one came to care for them.

In the middle of the plot, Gabby had cleared a space to work, so the ground around the bare patch of earth was covered in a layer of leaves and litter from the surrounding forest. Pointing to the clear patch in the centre, she said, "Stand right there."

Liz grimaced, but stood in the middle of the clearing, the pile of leaves around her. "Okay... What now?"

It'd be better if she just showed her, rather than try to explain what she could do. Raising her hands, Gabby concentrated on the leaves surrounding her friend. She was aiming for something a little less scary than starting a wildfire—something beautiful.

Gabby felt the familiar tingle as her power hummed through her fingertips and the leaves began to twitch before rising slowly into the air. Liz's expression fell into shock as they rose higher, floating all around.

"Gabby," she breathed, turning around and poking a leaf. She watched it spin in the air with wide eyes, a smile spreading across her face. "This is incredible. How...?"

Gabby shrugged, dropping her hands, and the leaves fell back to the ground with a flutter. "I guess I'm a witch."

"You guess?"

"I suppose so."

"What else can you do?"

"Small things. I can light tiny fires, like a candle. I can sense things like animals and people..."

Liz stared at her with a look of wonder. "How is that possible?"

"Your guess is as good as mine." Gabby had no idea, but all she was certain of was that she could do it and it was getting stronger every single day.

"How does it even work?"

"There are spells and that kind of thing, but mostly, I just feel it. If I concentrate hard enough, it just happens."

"This is... I don't even know."

"I have no idea what I'm doing. It's all been trial and error so far."

Liz glanced at the ground, her forehead creased like she was trying to think something through. Probably trying to decide the best route to the loony bin.

"I don't know how much help I can be," her friend said after an agonising minute. "But we can figure it out together."

Gabby's heart warmed with the thought of having such an amazing friend. "We need to keep this a secret, Liz. You can't tell anyone. Not even Alex."

"Who else knows?" she asked, stepping forwards.

"No one. Just you."

Liz frowned before circling her arms around her friend and squeezing her in a hug. "Thank you for trusting me."

time to start fresh. What use was immortality if they spent it in agony?

There was a shift in the humid air around them and Sam frowned at the promise of a new complication. Perhaps they weren't as alone here as they first thought.

"Did you feel that?" Zac asked, turning to look out across the lake at their backs.

"Yeah." He'd recognised it instantly. *Witches.*

"I'm going to check it out."

"Zac," he said, "leave it. It's more trouble than it's worth."

"If we're gonna move back in, little brother, then I want to know who's sacrificing cute fluffy baby animals in our backyard, don't you?" He rose an eyebrow at him and before Sam could retort, he'd disappeared.

It was always the same with his big brother. Dive in headfirst, cause a scene, *then* ask questions. It was like he was punishing the entire world because he didn't have a choice when it came to his fate.

With a groan, Sam followed him through the forest and realised that the ripple of power he'd felt was coming from the cemetery. It was quiet, isolated, and was the perfect place to work undetected— unless, of course, if there was someone like them listening.

He stopped just inside the tree line and watched Zac, who stood in the middle of the clearing, towering over the witch who was sitting cross-legged in the middle of their family plot.

She was young, early twenties perhaps, all wild hair and olive complexion. Her eyes snapped open and when she realised she wasn't alone, she scrambled to her feet with a cry. It was then he realised she must be new at this, extremely new.

"Well, well, well... what do we have here?" Zac asked, coming to life.

"Leave her alone, Zac." He stepped out of the tree line a little too quickly and the witch jumped again. He looked her over and frowned. The girl's heart was beating a million miles a minute.

Zac rolled his eyes. "I wasn't going to eat her, brother, if that's what you're thinking. I don't want her to point her witchy juju at me."

"Y-you're b-both d-dead," the witch stammered, stumbling back another step.

"As a doornail," Zac said with a grin.

"Forgive my brother," Sam said, stepping forwards. Best to put himself in front of his troublemaker of a brother before he got any ideas. "I think you know what we are. We can't hide from you, but we mean you no harm."

"Vampires," she said, finally realising.

"Ten points to Glinda." Zac clapped theatrically.

"Glinda?"

"From *The Wizard of OZ*," he replied. "I'm trying to be *nice*, but it gives me heartburn."

"Ignore him," Sam said, rolling his eyes. "The moron is my brother Zac."

Zac smirked. "Stupid is as stupid does."

"*Zac*," he scolded.

"What?"

Sam turned back to the witch. "We own the manor across the lake."

"The Degaud manor?" she asked, her body still tense like she was waiting for them to pounce on her.

"It's our family home, so yeah, it's ours," Zac said with a scowl.

"You're... But there's no Degaud's left."

"We've got a smart one here."

"Zac." Sam pushed his brother back a step. "We want to live amongst you," he explained. "This was where we lived our human lives, and we want to reconnect with our humanity."

She glanced over her shoulder nervously. "Why?"

"Let's just say it helps with... you know." He absently waved his hand, hoping she would get it. "What's your name?"

She eyed them suspiciously, still undecided about their intentions. Zac hadn't helped, what with his typical attitude problems.

"Gabrielle," she replied slowly. "Gabby."

"We don't want to cause any trouble, Gabby," Sam said. "We hope that we can be friends—"

"If you do anything to hurt anyone in the town, especially my family and friends, I'll make you pay." She cast her gaze onto Zac and scowled. "Especially you."

"I'm in love," Zac retorted, making a kissy face at her.

Gabby narrowed her eyes at him, and Sam felt the air thicken. It was the mark of an unskilled witch; usually they could never sense it coming, and he didn't know which one was worse. As her spell hit him, Zac fell to his knees with a gasp that would no doubt hurt his pride in more ways than one. Grasping his head in his hands, he let out a groan.

"I always wanted to try that one." She smirked down at his brother.

Looking at his brother, who still had his head in his hands, Sam tried his best not to laugh, wondering how many brain cells the newbie witch had just exploded.

"I know, I know," his brother said with a grimace, "I told you so."

Liz's feet hit the pavement hard as she ran, earphones stuck in her ears, trying to block out the world around her. Running was her thing. It cleared her mind and allowed her to think. Running was her alone time.

It'd been a week since Gabby had dragged her out into the middle of the old cemetery and shown her the impossible. Her best friend was a witch. A real live witch! Liz would've said stranger things had happened, but that was as strange as it got. Not even a ten-mile run could help her work out that one.

She was a block from her apartment when she slowed to a jog, her mind still full to bursting with magic. When she rounded the corner, she smacked right into a brick wall and cried out in alarm. She stumbled back a step, her earphones falling out of her ears. A pair of firm hands grasped her shoulders and she realised she'd been so distracted that she'd smacked right into a man walking in the other direction.

"Whoa," the guy said, holding her steady. "Careful there."

Looking up, her gaze met the most swoon-worthy set of green eyes she'd ever seen in her entire life.

"Are you okay?" the guy asked, a frown creasing his forehead. He looked about her age and stood a head taller than she did.

"Um, yeah," she muttered, looking away, realising she'd been staring at him like some kind of idiot.

He was hot. Like, there were hot guys and then there were *hot guys*. He was in the latter category. Amazing eyes, short brown hair, chiseled jawline, hard chest... Definitely hot.

Why the hell did she have to be all sweating and gross in her running gear right now? It was like the universe had conspired against her. The guy was still looking at her, a grin pulling at his lips. Ugh, she was staring again.

"Are you sure you're okay?" he asked with a chuckle.

"Yeah. I'm fine," she retorted, growing irritated. "You just surprised me."

"Sorry about that." He shuffled from foot to foot. "I'm Sam."

"Liz."

"I just moved here with my brother. Nice place."

"Why would you want to move here?" She was trying her best to get out.

Sam laughed and ran a hand through his hair. "It's as good a place as any. Helps that we own a house here."

He had money and was hot. Nice combination. "You own a house?"

"Yeah," he said like it was the most normal thing in the world—a guy who didn't look a day older than twenty owning a house. "The plantation manor over by the lake."

"The Degaud manor?" Her mouth almost dropped open. Nobody had lived there since the Civil War—since the alleged massacre.

"Yeah. I know what you locals think of the place, that it's haunted, but I haven't seen a ghost yet." He winked and it almost melted her insides.

"But nobody's been in there since—"

"The Civil War."

"Yeah."

"Well, it's our family's ancestral home, so you know."

"You're a Degaud?" she asked, letting her surprise show.

Sam nodded slowly, tilting his head to the side.

"It's just..." Liz began, "there hasn't been any Degauds around here since the place was abandoned."

"Well, some are still alive and kicking," he said with a laugh. "Where are you going? Liz..."

"Evans." She gestured to her clothes and pointed down the street. "I'm going home to change. Then I'm going to work."

He looked her over, letting his gaze slowly drag over her body and despite herself, she shivered. "Well, I won't keep you. It was nice meeting you, Liz. I'm sure we'll *run* into each other at some stage."

She snorted. "Very funny."

"I do my best."

As he stepped around her and continued down the sidewalk, she called out after him, "Nice meeting you, too."

When he glanced back and caught her checking out the rear view, she turned away, her cheeks flushing.

It'd been a crazy week. First, Gabby and her amazing witch abilities and now, a hot guy to drool over… and he was a Degaud no less! A Degaud with a *brother*. Damn, she was in trouble.

If there was one thing Zac was good at, it was sniffing out the closest bar.

The only place that seemed to exist in a twenty-mile radius was a hole called *Max's*. It seemed to be part *TGI Friday's* mixed with a dose of rough biker bar. It didn't matter either way—if they served alcohol, he was there.

Setting himself up at one end of the bar, he settled in for the long haul. A glass of scotch wasn't anywhere near adequate so he bought the bottle and kept topping up when it got low. Never mind it was only four p.m. and not even dinnertime.

Zac drank enough booze to send any normal human to the hospital ten times over, but it never seemed to be enough. Control was something that was constantly out of his grasp, and he wasn't talking about the drinking. The thing about being a vampire who was turned against his will was that he was never taught or never learned when to start or stop.

He died in the Civil War like some kind of cliché, was turned when he was as good as dead, and taught to hunt and kill the people he used to share DNA with. And then there was Sam. It was his fault his little brother was turned and he paid for it every day. It took every ounce of his willpower not to chow down on the population of Ashburton, the town they once called home—the town they wanted to call home again.

Scratch that. The town *Sam* wanted to become human in again and as usual, Zac was along for the ride. Did he want the same thing? He wasn't human anymore. Hadn't been for a very long time.

Zac Degaud was the definition of the word monster.

He caught movement out of the corner of his eye as someone came up to the bar near where he'd set up residence. He straightened when he got a whiff of something tasty. Something *female* and tasty.

"What'll it be, Liz?" the bartender asked.

"Gimme some of those amazing fries and a jug of beer."

"Comin' right up."

Zac watched the girl out of the corner of his eye as she waited for her order, and as expected, she glanced his way, giving him the once over. She wore those little denim shorty shorts that women were so fond of this decade and a cream-coloured blouse. When her gaze met his, he stared. There were blue eyes, then there were hers.

"Hey, I'm sorry to stare," she began, turning to face him, "but you kinda look familiar."

"I don't think so," he said with a smirk, swivelling the stool around to face her. *Familiar or hot?* "I just moved here with my brother."

"Brother?"

"Sam, the high and mighty. Maybe you've seen his colossal head."

"Oh, Sam? Sam Degaud?"

Zac snorted. He had to give it to his little brother. He worked fast.

"Yes, I've met him," she added. "This morning."

Zac was tall and lean with a head of messy brown hair. Sam was more heavy-set than he was, and his hair was a shade or two lighter, but they shared the same green eyes and bone structure. Simple way of putting it, they looked like brothers.

"Really?" he asked.

"I didn't know there were any Degauds left. I mean, any that were related to the founding family."

"Well, there's two of us." He took another mouthful of scotch to soothe the burning that was rising in his throat. She really did smell that good.

"I'm Liz," she said, holding out her hand.

Zac let his gaze drop and wondered if he should touch her. That'd be dangerous, considering he was already wondering what her blood tasted like. It was getting to the point of awkward, so he held his breath and took her hand.

"Zac Degaud. Older brother. *Bad boy.*"

"Oh, so you're one of those." She laughed as he held her hand for a moment too long.

"This is your first warning," he said, his lips curving into a lopsided grin.

Pulling her hand away, Liz laughed, shaking her head, but he knew different. Her heart had sped up slightly and his already massive ego inflated to a bursting point.

The bartender came back at that moment, interrupting their interlude, and put her order on the bar in front of them.

Picking up her fries and jug of beer, she slid off the stool. "Well, I'll see you later."

Zac swivelled around on the stood and watched her walk across the room. *Damn.*

"Well, I can see you're working fast, as per usual."

Zac looked up and found Sam sliding onto the stool on his other side and shrugged. "A bar and a pretty girl. You know what I'm like."

Sam glared at him. "She—"

"Smells nice?" Zac asked with a grin.

"Get lost."

"Helps that she's pretty, too."

"Don't you dare touch her, Zac, or I'll—"

Turning in his seat, Zac narrowed his eyes in warning. "Or you'll *what*?"

Sam let out a sharp sigh. "Just don't cause any trouble. I want to settle here. Don't ruin it before it has even begun."

"Let me guess." Zac tapped his temple, pretending to think. "You saw her first, so this is your way of saying 'hands off'? You know you can just say hands off, right?"

"I'm getting some contractors out at the manor tomorrow, so keep clear, okay?"

"Subtle change of topic, Samuel."

Sam's jaw tensed, but he didn't rise to the bait. "It's the difference between no hot water and electricity, so just play along."

Zac shrugged and turned back to his scotch.

"I'm going home... and Zac?"

When he didn't reply, his little brother shoved his shoulder. "What?"

"No eating the locals."

Before he could retort, Sam was striding across the bar, giving a little wave to Liz as he went. Since when had his little brother become his parent?

That's when he realised Liz wasn't alone. Probably served him right, fixating on the first pretty girl to cross his path. He watched that newbie witch, Gabby, talking with her and rolled his eyes. Tabitha was friends with the girl? *Figured.*

When the witch turned and caught his eye, she scowled. Giving her a little wave, she rolled her eyes and turned back to Liz. Zac cast his hearing out, already knowing exactly what they were talking about.

"I'll be right back," Gabby said and a moment later, he felt her approach. This place was suddenly extremely aggravating.

"Stay away from her," Gabby hissed in his ear.

Zac took another mouthful of his scotch before raising an eyebrow at her. "Or you'll make my head explode?"

"I'll do more than that."

"I can smell a bluff a mile off, Tabitha, so save yourself the hassle and go back to the minor leagues. Something tells me you can't cut it in the majors."

"Eat shit."

"Eat shit?" He laughed, slapping his hand on top of the bar. "Kids these days."

"You keep your filthy fangs to yourself, Zac Degaud, or I'll rip them out myself."

Downing the rest of his drink, he got up from his stool and leaned in close to the witch's ear and whispered, *"Try me, Glinda."*

He felt the telltale hum in the air that signalled

the newbie witch was about to get all voodoo on his ass.

Eyeing her, he said, "Gabrielle Marie Cohen. Twenty years old. Works as a clerk over at the real estate agency across the square. Lives at the top of that eyesore of an apartment block on Sycamore. Crazy absentee grandmother, who I'm guessing was a witch who had her secret exposed. Parents, Judith and Thomas. Mommy is a teacher at Ashburton Primary. Daddy dearest is a lawyer at *Everton and Cootes Legal* in Baton Rouge. They live over on Everton Street, right?"

"Asshole."

"Meh," he said with a shrug. "It's called insurance, sweetheart. You make my head pop, I make someone else's pop right off."

"Leave Liz alone."

"Look at you getting all territorial and foamy at the mouth."

"Screw you, Zac."

"No thanks, brunettes aren't my type."

"She doesn't know what you are and it's staying that way. You don't touch her *and* you don't even look at her, understand?"

"I don't think you understand what a threat entails, little witch."

Gabby crossed her arms over her chest. "I'm calling your bluff."

"I love a dare," he snarled. "Push too far, Gabby, and I'll push back ten times as hard. You really want to play this game with me?"

"The next time you go near Liz, we'll see who's really bluffing then, won't we?"

Zac's lips curved into a wicked grin as his blood quickened. He loved living life on the edge. A newbie witch versus a one-hundred- and seventy-year-old vampire with a blonde beauty as the prize.

"Bring it on, Tabitha. Bring. It. On."

CHAPTER 3

Three weeks in Ashburton and Zac still felt as pathetic as he always did. It was a hole of a town filled with nothing and nobody—except maybe a certain blonde human who was nice to look at. Three weeks wasn't very long in the grand scheme of his afterlife, but as always, impatience ruled.

He'd lost count of how many times he'd got into fisticuffs with some guy whose girlfriend had wandering eyes, or rednecks who thought it was their duty to beat him up because he was new in town. It was always the same wherever he went. Trouble followed and he was happy to show it his fists. No prizes for guessing who came out the other side victorious. Their blood always tasted like crap.

"Hey."

Zac looked up from his regular spot at the bar and grinned when he saw a pair of blue eyes looking back at him. "Hey."

"You certainly are the booze hound, aren't you?" Liz asked, nudging his bottle of Jack Daniels with a finger.

"Where some people like a fine wine, I prefer the hard stuff." He winked and ran his tongue across his bottom lip.

"What's your game?" she asked, sliding onto the stool next to him.

"My game? I have no game."

"Are you the same Zac Degaud who's beat up every tough guy in town?"

He rose his eyebrows and flashed her a wicked grin. "I told you day one, beautiful. Bad boy."

"So, is this my second warning?"

"Are we only at two? I'm slipping."

When Liz laughed, her entire face lit up. "I think we can skip the warnings, I get it."

He felt his cold, dead skin warm. "Do you want a drink? I'm buying."

"I'm going to have to say no," she said, glancing over her shoulder. "I'm meeting Gabby."

"Ahh," he said. "Blown off for a girl." *Otherwise known as Glinda the good witch. Or more aptly* described as the annoying as hell witch who still didn't have the guts to call her bluff.

"Yeah, sorry." Waving across the room, she threw a smile back at him. "See you later."

When Liz turned away, he made a kissy face at Gabby, who'd just walked into the bar and was throwing daggers with her eyes. Tapping his temple, she turned away and greeted her friend like nothing was wrong. *Witches.*

Not wanting to suffer Gabby's presence, he downed the rest of his bottle of Jack and strode across the bar and out into the darkness. The street was lit in an orange glow from the streetlamps, the gardens across the road bathed in a thick layer of black. Truth was, this entire place stunk of a life he'd never get back.

It wasn't boredom, it wasn't like he couldn't find anything interesting to do... he just didn't like the reminders that were everywhere. He was a failure who got his entire family killed and he was the reason his brother was a blood-sucking parasite. *Good job, Zac Degaud. You should've stayed dead that time you got shot in the gut. You should've asphyxiated on your own blood, embraced the darkness, and never woke up.*

Grimacing, he turned to start the long walk back to the manor, otherwise known as the scene of the crime. Rounding the corner, he came face to face with last night's conquest. Three big, beefy rednecks otherwise known as stupid one, stupid two, and stupid three, who just didn't get when to walk away.

"Oh, hey," he drawled, coming to a stop in front of them. "Didn't you get the message when I beat your asses into the pavement the first time?"

"You only get to beat my ass once, Degaud," the biggest, plaid-clad idiot snarled. "Once and never again."

"Oh, I'm going to have fun with this." Zac laughed as the human stepped forwards, his friends egging him on.

The redneck took a swing, and for good measure, Zac let the guy's fist connect with his nose. The humans let out a holler as blood dripped over his lips and onto his brand-new black shirt. Damn. If there was one thing he hated, it was doing laundry. Bloodstains were the worst.

Feeling his teeth ache at the taste of his own blood, Zac said, "I was going to be nice and let you get in a few before I snapped you all in half, little boy, but you just ruined my new shirt."

Moving faster than the human men could follow, Zac's fist connected with a temple, dropping one before turning to the second, grinding his face into the pavement before turning back to the guy who'd given him his bloody nose.

"*Shit*," the guy hissed, realising he was on his own.

"Shit, indeed." Zac grabbed the guy's shoulder and rammed a fist into his stomach before shoving him up against the wall, cracking his head against the brickwork. It must have split his skin because the sickly scent of blood filled his nose.

Letting him go, Zac stepped back a few steps and gestured the guy forwards, bouncing from foot to foot. "C'mon," he said. "Give it your best shot."

The human took a swing with an impressive roar, but Zac grabbed his wrist, shoving him against the opposite wall, drawing more blood.

"Is that all you've got? *Go again.*"

"Asshole," the human snarled, rubbing his nose and smearing blood across his face.

"Why, yes, I believe I am."

The guy lunged again, but it wouldn't do him any good. Zac could see every move coming a mile off. He'd seen it all in his one hundred and seventy years, and even without his speed and strength, he'd get out of this fight the same way. Stupidity bred stupidity and dumb brawn who didn't know their left from right.

Sick of fighting, Zac downed the guy with a single blow. The human clutched his head and fell heavily onto the pavement, groaning in agony. The stench of blood filled his senses and grabbing the front of the human's shirt, he lifted him from the ground, letting his eyes change into complete darkness. Scary vampire, *check*.

"Zac."

Rolling his eyes at the sudden appearance of his little brother, Zac let the guy go, doing nothing to cushion his fall back to the asphalt.

"Again?" Sam exclaimed, surveying the ass whooping he'd just delivered to the latest group of heroes who dared cross his path.

"I didn't start this one, just so you know. I was defending my honour." He smirked, holding up his hands. "They taste like shit, so wipe that look off your face, little brother. I wouldn't eat that even if you paid me."

"Compel them and let them go."

"Aww, I was just getting started." He wiped his nose with the back of his hand. "I even let them get a few swings in for good measure."

"If you want to fight someone, fight me."

"As if you could take me."

"Maybe not but taking your boredom out on innocent humans isn't the way to find constructive entertainment."

"Innocent?" Zac scoffed. "They're far from squeaky clean."

"I thought you wanted to change, Zac? Or did you forget whatever it was that happened to you in Vietnam?"

Zac had fought in every war since he'd died, and what for? A constructive way to feed his bloodlust? An excuse to go on killing?

"I thought you didn't want to be a monster anymore." Sam glared at him, daring him to snap. "So why are you still acting like it?"

"You know what?" Zac sniffed, glancing towards the opposite end of the lane. "Clean it up yourself."

Before Sam could retort, he disappeared into the darkness.

***

"Is there anything you want to tell me?" Gabby asked, smirking at Liz across the table.

It was their weekly ritual to meet at *Max's* and gossip. For such a small town, a lot happened, but not as much since the Degaud brothers moved into the old plantation manor.

Liz might know she was a witch, but there was no way she'd let on that they were vampires. It was a dangerous step into the supernatural world she wasn't willing to let her friend take. The more Liz knew, the more trouble she'd get into. Liz was destined to get into college and move far, far away and as her best friend, it was Gabby's duty to make sure she was happy.

That meant not finding out that vampires existed.

"Tell you what?" Liz asked, picking up a fry coated with a thick layer of cheese. "That I'm consuming too much fat? That I'll have to run an extra mile tomorrow to make up for it?"

Laughing, Gabby kicked her friend under the table. "No... but yeah. I demand one extra mile tomorrow."

"You've got it."

"Seriously, you've been spending a lot of time with Sam."

"He's nice. Nothing like his brother." She sighed, playing with a napkin.

"Liz."

"What?" she asked, straightening up.

"Don't tell me..."

"Don't tell you what?"

"You like both of them." Liz's cheeks flushed and she knew she had it bang on the money. "Liz!"

She shrugged. "You say it like it's a bad thing."

"It is, considering one of them is the biggest asshole in town."

"Hell, Gabby. They're both so good-looking and all the flirting…"

Gabby eyed her friend. "Damn, Liz. You've got it bad."

"I'm expecting a letter from one of the colleges I've applied to any day and now they show up. Talk about throwing a spanner in the works."

"Liz, don't let a guy you hardly know determine your entire future."

"I wouldn't," she said with a wicked smile. "It'd just be a little fun. God knows I need some."

Gabby's face split into a grin. "I'd go for door number one…"

"Sam?"

"Shit, yeah."

If she was going to push her friend towards any of the brothers, it'd be Sam. He was the only one who'd remained true to his word and had not caused any trouble with the human population. Zac had done nothing but drink himself stupid and fight anyone who looked at him twice. Then there was the issue of her best friend dating a vampire and not knowing about it, but if Liz couldn't be persuaded otherwise… Sam was a better bet.

Catching Liz gazing over at Zac, she said, "Do

you think Zac would treat you with the respect you deserve? He'd think you were his possession, and it would be nice for a while—"

"I get it, Gabby," Liz interrupted. "You're Team Sam."

"Damn straight. He gets an A-plus for respect... and an F for longevity."

Liz just shook her head, her gaze following Zac, who'd vacated his spot by the bar and was pushing through the exit.

"Don't let yourself fall for them. *Seriously.*"

Liz rolled her eyes and picked up another fry. "Hardly."

But from the look on Liz's face, Gabby knew that wasn't going to happen, not by a long shot. Looked like she'd have to have words with the vampires yet again. Calling Zac's bluff would blow.

The next morning, Liz sat on the grass in the middle of Ashburton's Botanical Gardens, playing with her cellphone. No letter. No email. All this waiting was killing her.

"Hey."

Glancing up from her cell, she saw Sam looking

down at her, his hands shoved deep into his pockets, and her heart fluttered.

"Hey yourself."

"Mind if I join you?" he asked, gesturing to the patch of grass next to her.

"Sure."

He sunk down next to her, stretching his long legs out in front of him. She couldn't help but give him the once over, thankful her sunglasses shielded her eyes.

"Day off?" Sam asked with a slight smirk, giving away that she hadn't been as covert as she thought.

"Yeah," she said with a small laugh. "There isn't much to do around here, hence sitting in the gardens."

He shrugged. "It's as good a place as any."

"It's been a few weeks since you moved, right?"

"Three."

"You must do something? I mean, you didn't come here just to live in that big old house, did you?"

"No." He shook his head with what looked like a tinge of sadness, but she wasn't sure if she should ask.

"Then what do you do?"

"I walk," he said. "It helps me think. I'm not sure what I want to do."

"That's why I run. I mean, for the thinking."

Looking away so he wouldn't see her expression, she rolled her eyes. Could she be any more awkward?

Sam laughed. "It sure does clear the mind."

"Do you have a job?" *Did he need one?*

"No." He shook his head. "No job."

"Then why don't you try for one?"

He shrugged, casting his gaze across the gardens. Whenever she ran into him, he'd always been here, amongst the flowerbeds or wandering the paths. When she ran, she took a route that led her through town, into the forest by the edges of the swamp, and to the bayou beyond. Always on well-worn paths and always in daylight hours. There was something about the solitude of nature that allowed her to think—especially the wildness of the South. Maybe Sam felt the same.

"If you're looking for a job, they're hiring here in the gardens." Her cheeks flushed as she realised he probably didn't want to sink to the lowly position of gardener, even if he enjoyed walking here. What the hell was she thinking? "But you're probably looking for something more... collar and tie."

"No," Sam said, shaking his head. "It sounds great. God knows I need some simplicity right now."

"Oh."

"It just with renovating the manor and dealing with Zac. It's just a handful, you know."

"Your brother seems to like getting into trouble. The rumour mill is already turning." Apparently, Zac had gotten into a fight again last night after he'd left the bar. She'd already heard it from three people between her house and work. At least they finally had something else to talk about other than her lack of college plans and husband. Like that was front-page news. She'd fallen back to page ten since the Degaud brothers moved to town.

Sam let out a lengthy sigh. "He's my brother and I love him, but he's just... lost, I guess. Acting out."

She frowned. "I guess he just hasn't found what he's looking for."

"I guess."

Thinking that a change in topic was called for, she said, "If you're interested in that job, I can introduce you to Alex. He's doing everything on his own at the moment and could really use the help. I'm sure he could put a good word in for you."

"Alex? You're friends with him?"

Liz wondered if she'd just detected a hint of jealousy in his voice and felt her heart begin to speed up. "Yeah. I've known him since forever. We're good friends."

"Okay. That sounds good."

They sat in silence for a while, the sun beating down on their shoulders. It was strange how they kept running into each other, not that she minded. Talking with Sam was nice. He seemed to get her, which was more than she could say for his brother. Where Zac was concerned, she wasn't sure who he was at all. That man seemed hell-bent on keeping everyone at arm's length.

Sam shifted, bringing her attention back onto him. "What about you? I know you work at that café across the street. Surely, that's not all you want to do with your life?"

Liz sighed and grimaced at the same old question everyone asked her. Small-town girl wanting to make a big town life.

"Did I ask the wrong question?"

"No, it's just... After I graduated high school, everyone wanted me to go off to a fancy college and have this high-flying career, but I didn't know what I wanted."

"So, you stuck around until you could figure it out?"

She turned and gave him a pointed look. "Yeah. Exactly."

"Have you decided yet?"

"I applied to a bunch of colleges a few months back, but I haven't heard yet. The waiting is killing me."

"I'm sure you'll hear something soon."

She smiled at his reassurance.

"Listen," he began a little awkwardly. "I hope I'm not being too upfront here, but I was wondering if you wanted to do something later?"

The way he hesitated warmed her heart. "Like a date?"

"Yeah," he laughed, "like a date."

Smiling, she watched him for a moment. "Yeah. I'd like that."

⸺

Sam leaned against the doorframe, watching Zac sprawled out on the sofa. He'd claimed the parlour in the manor as his drinking hole from the day they'd arrived. If he wasn't at the bar, then he was here, but tonight he had to go somewhere else.

"I thought you'd be at the bar," Sam said.

"Nope."

"Can you go someplace else?"

"You've got a date, haven't you?" Zac sat up, suddenly interested.

"Don't you have a bottle of hooch to down?" he asked with a scowl.

Zac just grinned at him with a knowing look in his eyes. "You're bringing her here, aren't you?"

"It's none of your business."

"It's my business if you want to chow down on some pretty blonde in our house. Especially since you forbid me to do it... *Dad*."

Anger boiled beneath his skin and Sam felt his vampire side awaken. Hell if he was going to give Zac the satisfaction. "I'm not going to feed from her, Zac. I wouldn't—"

"*You like her.*"

"And what's your game, huh? I know you've been harassing her."

"Harassing?" Zac stood, crossing the room so they stood face to face.

Great, Sam thought, *another fight.*

"I can't talk to anyone without it being anything but harassment?" his brother asked.

"I'm not in the mood to fight with you, Zac. Just do me a favour, and go someplace else for tonight. Just one night."

"Then who's going to stop you if you can't stop yourself? Hmm? How long has it been since you've tasted human blood, brother? It's been forty years since I came back, and I haven't seen you consume a single drop."

He was right. It'd been decades since he'd fed from a human and if he got even a whiff of Liz's blood, he wouldn't be able to control himself. Especially considering the feelings she was stirring up inside him. What a way to find out that he was a vampire.

"I'm not going to feed from her, Zac."

"*Whatever*. The witch had words with me today, just so you know."

"You're the only one she has a problem with."

"You'll have a problem if Liz doesn't turn up for work tomorrow, little brother."

Sam gritted his teeth. "I can handle myself, Zac. I wouldn't do anything to hurt her."

"So says you."

Shoving Zac's shoulder, he snapped, "I say it."

"Fine, fine," Zac said, holding his hands up. "Don't come crying to me when you want to get the stains out of the carpet." He picked up the half-empty bottle of spirits he'd left on the coffee table and shoved past Sam, their shoulders clashing. When the front door slammed closed, he sighed in relief.

Sam didn't believe Zac for one second. There wasn't anything in the world that would make him hurt Liz. *Nothing*. He couldn't deny that over the past few weeks his feelings had grown. Feelings he wasn't sure he could have anymore, especially for a human girl. He wasn't sure what he was doing, but he knew he couldn't stay away.

Despite the dangerous path he was taking, he

smiled when he heard her car pull up in the driveway. He was at the front door in a flash. Taking a deep breath, he put on his human face before opening it, revealing Liz with her fist hovering in mid-air.

"I was just about to knock," she said with a nervous laugh. "I swear."

"I know," he replied. "I heard your car." They stood awkwardly for a moment, just staring at each other before he stepped back with a chuckle. "Come in."

"Wow," she said, stepping by him in a cloud of jasmine perfume and something distinctively human. "Some place you've got here."

"Thanks," he replied, thankful she wasn't facing him. He was sure his face betrayed his rising... hunger. "Can I get you anything? A drink?"

"No, I'm okay. I'm more interested in seeing inside the infamous Degaud manor." Catching his raised eyebrow, she added, "And you, of course. It's just that no one's been inside here in about a hundred years. I was wondering if it was still habitable."

"One hundred and forty-eight years," he corrected.

Liz pulled her gaze from the house and frowned at him.

"Or so say the records," he added lamely. "C'mon. I'll give you the grand tour."

He led her long the hallway, pointing out the paintings along the walls, all seventieth century French portraits of long lost Degauds and landscapes of the old country. The old country being France.

"You'll have to forgive the kitchen," he said, showing her in. "We've still got a lot of work to do."

He watched her look over the mess the builders had left after they'd finished work that afternoon. Ladders, tools, and sawdust sat over drop sheets, half the cabinets still needed installing, and the plumbing was still days from being connected.

"It'll look great when it's done," she said, glancing back to him. "And just you and Zac live here?"

"Yes."

"All this space?" she asked.

"Yes. There's five bedrooms upstairs, one we've remodelled into a second bathroom, so there's four now..."

"Wow, you've really got it planned out. What about the outside?"

"We can't do anything to the exterior, but we're free to update the interior to a certain point. We've been wiring electricity, replacing the plumbing, and modernising the bathrooms. The furniture and paintings are heirlooms, so we won't touch those."

"It's very... French."

"My family originated from France, so it would be," he said with a wink.

"You do have a strange accent. Not quite Southern..."

"Ahh, well, we've spent a lot of time away, so that would probably explain it." She was rather observant. Back then, there was Southern and then there was French Southern. His accent was very much flavoured with his family's heritage. Most people didn't notice these days since it was more common to move around than it had been in the eighteen hundreds.

"And you're only twenty?"

The real number would probably give her palpitations. "Twenty-one."

"Wow."

"Wow?"

"I mean, it's a lot for someone who's so young."

"Old families have a lot of responsibility attached to them. Name, heritage, that kind of thing."

"Your parents are big on it, huh?" she asked, turning away from the landscape painting she was looking at in the dining room.

His parents? An image flashed in his mind—an

image from his last moments as a human. Blood, nothing but blood.

"Sam?" Liz was looking at him with a frown.

"My parents aren't around anymore." Because they weren't.

"I'm sorry. I didn't—"

He held up a hand to stop her. "It's okay. It's been a long time." He led her back into the parlour and watched as she sat on the sofa across from the open fireplace.

"So..." she began, sitting on her hands.

"Sorry," he said sitting beside her. "I'm not very good at this."

"Holding up a conversation?" She smiled at him, bumping her shoulder against his.

Leaning closer, he shook his head. "Holding a conversation with a beautiful woman."

"Oh."

She blushed and he reached out and tucked a loose strand of blonde hair behind her ear. When his fingertips brushed against her skin, she shivered slightly, leaning into his touch. Did she feel it, too? That... tingling? Vampires felt everything a million times worse than a human, but if she even felt an inkling of what he did...

Her big blue eyes dropped from his, focusing on his lips and before he lost his nerve, he leaned forward and caught her is a kiss. Soft, tentative, just a little bit of pressure. It was probably best to take it slow, considering what he was.

But Liz took him by surprise, winding her arms around his neck, fingers tangling in the hair at the nape of his neck, pulling him against her. She was the one in control, deepening the kiss, sliding her tongue against his and he was a goner.

When she pulled away, he didn't want to let her go.

"I've wanted to do that for a while now," he murmured, brushing her hair away from her face.

"You have?" she asked.

"Ever since you ran into me. *Literally*."

Pressing his lips against hers again, he knew Zac had been wrong. He'd never do anything to hurt Liz... because he was falling for her.

Wasn't that a dangerous thought?

CHAPTER 4

The air was calm as Liz ran her well-worn path through the forest towards the bayou. It was also heavy with moisture, but what was new? She'd lived with the humidity her entire life, so it didn't bother her. Besides, there were other things on her mind, so the only thing to do was run. If she didn't, then all she'd be doing was fantasising about Sam all day. Damn, he was an excellent kisser—good as in mind-blowing.

When she saw a man standing on the path ahead, it didn't register at first. When it did, her heart tumbled in her chest and she skidded to a stop.

He looked rough around the edges—unshaven, clothing torn and dirty, mud caked into the knees of his jeans. There was this awful look of satisfaction on his face, like he'd been waiting for someone to come along the path... *someone like her.*

Her heartbeat sped up and her hands began to tremble. She was in trouble. *Big trouble.*

Bad things hardly happened in Ashburton—it was that kind of small, tight-knit community—but that didn't mean anything. Bad things could happen anywhere.

Spinning on her heel, she intended to bolt back the way she'd come, but when her gaze focused on another two men stepping between the trees and onto the path, she gasped, her heart wrenching painfully in her chest.

Making a split-second decision, she made a break for the tree line directly to her left, but she didn't make it far. She was grabbed from behind and pushed into the ground, face first. Pain burst through her cheek as the air was pushed out of her lungs.

"Where are they?" the first man asked, his voice raspy like he'd had one too many stiff drinks.

"Who?" she gasped, trying to struggle as he grabbed her hair, pulling her face towards his. He stunk like he'd rolled in something dead and she gagged.

"The vampers. Where are they?"

"What? I don't und—" She was yanked to her feet, her hair tearing painfully against her scalp.

"Lying *bitch*." The man shoved her into a set of arms that stunk just as bad. "Give her a taste of what we do to lying little human bitches."

Liz was helpless as the third man's hand connected with her temple, her head snapping to the side. Stars burst in her vision and the warm trickle of blood ran down her skin.

"*Let me go*," she shrieked, thrashing against her attackers.

Her arms were held behind her back, but she kicked her heel backwards, connecting with flesh. Suddenly, her arms were free, and she slipped between the men and ran.

Fear overtook her and she hardly knew which direction she was headed. Sounds of pursuit were coming from behind, but she couldn't focus on anything but her heaving breaths and thumping heartbeat.

Help. *She needed help.*

Another man she hadn't seen stepped into her path and she slammed into his chest, falling flat on her back. Staring up at the treetops, she couldn't make her limbs work.

No! No, this can't be happening to me.

"Help!" she screamed, thrashing as hands started to grab at her. "Help!"

"No one's coming, little bitch."

She stared up into the inhuman, beady eyes of her attackers and screamed.

It was no secret Sam liked to walk to clear his mind. Zac had his alcohol, but he had more constructive ways of dealing with his issues. Perhaps that job Liz was talking about at the gardens would help, too.

The forest had been oddly silent that morning. Usually there would be all kinds of sounds echoing through the trees. Birds playing in the Spanish moss that hung from cypress branches, the trickle of water from the river that fed into the lake, wind through the leaves overhead, but as he walked, everything was heavy and still. It kind of made his skin prickle.

That's when he caught the scent of werewolves on the air and scowled. Yet another complication to deal with.

They'd known there was a pack that lived deep in the bayou, but they were too far away to be an issue. If they were straying closer to Ashburton, then they'd caught onto the scent of vampires.

Damn it. He'd have to let Zac know when he got home, and when Zac smelled a fi—

A scream split the air and Sam's head snapped back towards the direction of the bayou. The sound was faint, far in the distance, but he ran anyway.

Suddenly, the forest was alive with noise. Not the soft, calm sounds he was used to, but the telltale signs of violence. If someone was in trouble, it was his duty to help, especially if the werewolves he'd smelled traces of earlier were harassing some poor girl.

Sam ran, but by the time he neared, whatever had happened to the woman was long over. Skidding to a stop, the scent of blood and wolves slammed into him and he almost doubled over, it was that strong. Holding his breath, he stepped out onto the forest path and saw a woman lying on her back covered in blood, her blue eyes glassy and vacant. He recognised her instantly and his heart leapt into his throat.

Liz.

God. Her blood was everywhere.

Her gaze seemed to fix on him, and she coughed, blood trickling from the corner of her mouth.

She was still alive.

He ran forwards and pulled her up into a sitting position. She cried out in pain and it was then he realised they were in big trouble. There was a reason she was covered in so much blood. The wolves had ripped her stomach open, and a steady stream of red was flowing, staining her top and the earth below.

"Liz, hold on, okay? It's okay..." But even as he said it, he knew it was too late.

She'd lost a lot of blood and her heart was already slowing... too slow to give her his blood. He was too late.

A tear slid down his cheek and he began to sob. The things he felt for this human girl were unexplainable.

Cradling her close, Sam held her as her eyes drooped and the life slowly bled from her. If they hadn't come back, then the werewolves wouldn't have come.

What was he going to do?

He murmured to her, telling it would be better soon, that it would stop hurting, that he was sorry. He smoothed her hair with his trembling fingers and stilled his tears.

He pressed his lips to her forehead, careful not to get the taste of blood in his mouth. He didn't want the last thing she saw to be the black eyes of a monster looking down on her.

When her heart slowed and finally stilled, he

crushed her limp body against his and felt his heart break.

It was all my fault.

This beautiful, vibrant woman had her entire life ahead of her. He should've left her alone. He should've been strong enough to stay away.

Her eyes snapped open and she gasped for air, hands clawing at his skin.

"Liz?" he cried, grasping her face with a steady hand, his heart beating as erratically as hers.

Willing her to focus and look at him, he pulled her towards him. She was alive? But her heart had been still, silent. That could only mean...

"No," he whispered, horrified. "Not you. *No...*"

"Sam?" Liz croaked.

Blood, there was too much blood. He checked the cuts on her face and arms, but they were already starting to fade. Tugging at her shirt, he saw the laceration in her abdomen was knitting itself back together.

Someone had changed her... *Who?*

"Sam?" she asked again, blood bubbling in her mouth, making her cough.

"You've had a nasty accident," he murmured, trying to hold his vampire side at bay. The last thing she needed was to see him change into something other than human.

She just stared up at him, her blue eyes that were usually so full of life, glassy.

"You're going to be okay," he said, pressing his lips to her forehead. "I'm going to take care of you, okay?"

"What—" she tried to ask, but it seemed like too much effort. No wonder, her body was working overtime to heal her wounds.

"Shh. Don't talk. I love you, okay? I'm going to take care of you."

She nodded so slightly, he almost missed it. Scooping her up in his arms, he frowned as her eyes fluttered and closed as she passed out.

He felt the tears stream down his face as he sprinted through the forest with her in his arms, running faster than he ever had in his entire life. He had to get her back to the manor. She would be safe there. Zac would know what to do... wouldn't he?

When he kicked open the front door, breaking the lock, he didn't understand how he'd gotten there. Striding down the hall, he didn't even register Zac, who was staring at him with a horrified expression.

What the hell must he look like? A bloodstained angel in the arms of a devil.

"What the hell, Sam?" Zac exclaimed, covering his nose and mouth with a hand.

"I found her in the forest," he said, hardly able to control himself.

"What did you do?" His brother moved forwards to take Liz from his arms, but he carried her up the stairs, ignoring Zac's accusation. "Sam? *What did you do?*"

Placing her gently on top of his bed, he ran his gaze over her bloodstained clothes. This wouldn't do.

"Sam," Zac said, trying to hold in his anger. "Did you give her your blood?"

"No!" He shoved his brother away. "I found her dying in the forest. I felt her heart stop, Zac. She was dead before I got there."

"She looks alive to me."

"I didn't do this to her. I would never—"

Zac placed a hand on his shoulder, but he couldn't tear his eyes from Liz. "I know you wouldn't, but I had to ask. You know I had to."

Sam nodded, his jaw tense. The stench of blood was still everywhere, and the stench of werewolves.

Zac took a deep breath and his gaze snapped to Liz, who was still out cold. "Sam?"

"Werewolves... Their scent was everywhere. Her stomach was ripped to shreds."

"I'll kill those dogs," Zac hissed.

"They must have picked up my scent on her and—"

Zac grasped his shoulders and shook him. "This isn't your fault, Sam. Not by a long shot. We need to get her out of those clothes. If she wakes up with all that blood on her..."

"I'll do it," Sam replied. "It'll be okay."

Zac seemed to sense he wasn't needed and grimaced. "If you say so." He turned to leave but stopped in the doorway. "Sam?"

He turned and met his brother's gaze for the first time since he'd walked into the manor.

"How did she get vampire blood in her system?"

"I don't know." He shook his head, numb. "I don't know."

Liz felt her eyes open, but it was a struggle. She felt heavy, like every limb was weighed down with lead. She was lying in a bed. A big, soft bed... Sam's bed?

The room was dark, only a sliver of light streamed through a slight crack in the curtains. Her vision focused even more, splitting her head in two. Everything was sharp... too sharp.

Reaching out towards the light, her fingers trailed through the stream and she pulled back with a hiss. Did the sun just burn her? She'd seen this on television before. People who were hypersensitive to light, touch, smell… What was happening to her?

"Liz?"

Turning her head, she saw Sam perched on the bed beside her. He looked worried. *What the hell was that smell?*

"It's okay," he murmured. "You had a nasty accident. It's going to be okay." He reached out and pressed a cool hand to her forehead, but it felt like his touch was burning through her skin.

"*Stop*," she cried, pushing him away.

Sam fell backwards, but instead of landing to the floor, he was halfway across the room. She stared at him, wondering how she could push a man twice her size with enough force to send him reeling.

"Liz," he said, sitting up into a crouch. "I don't know how to explain it to you, but you need to calm down—"

"Calm down?" she exclaimed, scrambling up against the headboard, her knees pulled into her chest.

"Yes. I'll explain everything—"

She slapped her hands over her ears, screwing her eyes shut. "Why do you have to yell at me?"

"I'm not," he told her. "You're different, Liz. You're changing."

"Changing? How did I get here, Sam? I was in the forest, then—" She halted, her eyes widening. She couldn't remember how she got here. She couldn't remember anything after she got to the six-mile mark in the forest near the bayou.

"I found you in the forest. You'd been attacked."

"Attacked?" She looked down at her bare legs, then turned her hands over and over. She was so cold...

"You don't remember?"

"Remember what?"

"Waking up in the forest?"

"I..." she trailed off, trying to sift through her memories. She was running, then... nothing.

"You died," he choked out. "I held you in my arms. You were dead."

"Dead?" Her heart constricted in on itself. But she was here, wasn't she?

"Then you woke up... Liz, I'm so sorry."

"You're sorry? If I died... Am I dead?"

"No." He shook his head. "You're changing, Liz."

She panicked. "Changing into what?"

"That's what I've been trying to tell you," he murmured, holding a hand out like he was trying to calm a wild animal. "I'm a vampire, Liz. Zac and I... we're vampires."

"What?" She looked at him like he was stark raving mad.

"And you're changing into one, too."

"You're lying. Why are you lying to me?" she cried, getting more and more agitated. "Let me go!"

She went to stumble out of the bed, but Sam stuck his thumb into his mouth. When he held it out to her, a bead of red blood swelled against his pale skin. A sickly-sweet smell filled every part of her, and she had to taste it. Lunging for him, he grasped her shoulders, holding her back. He grunted at the effort of holding her sudden fury at bay and pushed her onto the bed. He sucked his thumb into his mouth and suddenly, the smell was gone.

She slapped a hand over her mouth, embarrassed and dumbfounded at her reaction to... *blood*. She wanted it. She *needed* it.

"D-did you d-do this to me?" she stammered.

"No," he said. "I would never, ever change anyone. Neither would Zac. We never had a choice, Liz, so why would we force that onto someone else?"

Sam said nothing as she curled in on herself, her thoughts tumbling around and around like she was inside a washing machine.

Taking deep breaths, she hugged the blankets to her chest. The sun burned her skin, she wanted blood... Sam had to be at least a hundred and sixty years old. Who could live that long?

Finally, she looked up at him. "When you said your parents were dead, it was because of the time."

"No. It's not."

She just stared at him, not sure how to grasp onto anything that meant something.

"The vampire who turned Zac killed them, then turned me to get to him."

She hissed through her teeth and reached out for him. Somehow, she could understand he was telling the truth.

Sam didn't move, though. "He won't admit it, but Zac blames himself for me being this way. It wasn't his fault. It wasn't anyone's but the woman who did this to us."

"Do you think... Is she..."

"No. Zac killed her the night of the massacre."

"The massacre was real? It was vampires?"

"A single vampire, Liz. This isn't a game. None of what we do is. If you choose to complete the change, that is what you will become." His head dropped into his hands. "I'm so sorry. I'm so sorry this happened to you."

He began to sob and her heart swelled.

Creeping forwards across the mattress, Liz

threaded her arms around his strong back, laying her head against his shoulder. "I believe you."

He lifted his head. "How can you be so calm about this?"

Sighing, she tightened her embrace. "I have to be, don't I? I can hurt and lash out all I want, but it won't change the fact that I can't go back. I died. *I'm dead.* Isn't that some kind of miracle?"

"A miracle?" Sam scoffed. "A miracle would be a cure. A miracle would be turning you human again. A miracle would be having a *choice.*"

Sam never got a choice, she got that, but she did. It was just a heavier kind of decision. Life as a vampire or death. Maybe she was meant to die in the forest, maybe that was all the time she was meant to have. Or maybe she could live forever as something else. She couldn't fathom any of those options. All she knew was that she didn't want to die, but she wasn't sure she wanted to live on as a vampire, either.

Her, a vampire? The notion seemed so far-fetched, she snorted at the irony.

"You're wrong, Sam," she said, straightening. "I do have a choice."

"Liz—"

"How long do I have?"

"Please—"

"Sam." She squeezed her eyes closed and asked again. "How much time do I have?"

"Two days, maybe less." His voice came out at barely a whisper, but she heard it as clear as day. She was already different.

"Then I have to make a choice."

He cupped her face in his cool hands and she suddenly understood all the things that hadn't quite added up about him.

"You can't force me," she whispered, taking in his green eyes. Eyes that seemed a hundred times more luminescent than before.

"I would never force you to do something you didn't want, especially not this."

A tiny hint of a smile tugged at her lips. "I know."

To her surprise, he pressed his lips to hers and kissed her tenderly, a thumb stroking back and forth across her cheek.

"Can I get you anything?" he whispered when he pulled away.

"Can you call Gabby?" The emotions that welled up inside her were almost unbearable—love, despair, anger, longing. As much as she needed Sam, she needed her friend.

He nodded and rose from the bed, leaving Liz to figure out her fate on her own. She hoped Gabby would be able to help, because she didn't know what she was going to do.

When Gabby walked into Sam's room an hour later, Liz was fretting. She was feeling sicker by the minute. Was that how she was going to die if she didn't change? Waste away until she closed her eyes and didn't open them again?

Her friend almost ran across the room and threw herself on the bed, pulling her into a tight hug. "Hell, Liz."

"Screwed is a more appropriate word," she said wryly.

"How are you feeling?" Gabby asked.

"Like crap. Apparently, I was brutally attacked in the forest. I died and came back to life. My boyfriend is a vampire, and his brother is one, too. You're a witch. If I don't complete some kind of change, I will get sicker and die for real. If I go through it, I'll be a vampire. So yeah, I'm feeling great."

Maybe that was why she wasn't freaking out over the existence of vampires as much as she ought to. She knew Gabby was a witch, so this was the next logical step.

"I know," her friend said. "I know all about it. I

knew what the brothers were. I should've said something." The last part she said more to herself, but Liz only heard one thing. Her friend had known they were vampires. Real life vampires.

"You knew about them?" she asked, dumbfounded.

"I could tell what they were from day one."

"Why didn't you say anything?"

"Knowing I was a witch was crazy enough," she said, wringing her hands together. "They promised they wouldn't do anything to harm anyone and so far, they haven't."

"You pushed me towards Sam."

"He's good, Liz. He doesn't want to be a vampire. He never did. They came here to try to reconnect with their humanity. He's not a monster."

"But you pushed me towards him knowing what he was," she hissed.

"And if he tried anything, I would've dealt with him and his brother."

She shook her head. "How?"

"I'm a witch, Liz. I can make their brain cells explode and if it came to it, I think I've got the stomach to stake them... especially Zac."

"Stake them?" Liz felt sick. What had she become? What had her friend become?

"We don't live in the same world anymore, Liz.

It's screwed up and I don't like it, but things are different. I had to learn how to protect myself. I'm still learning."

"What about me? What happens if I want to change into—" She couldn't bring herself to say the word 'vampire'.

"Nothing will change between us, Liz. Nothing. You hear me?" Gabby grasped her friend's hands. "You're my best friend. I trust you with my life. Then and now. Whatever you choose."

She had to choose if she wanted to live or die. Twenty years old and she had to choose...

"I don't know what to do," she sobbed.

"I know."

"Did Sam tell you what happened in the forest? He said he found me, but I don't remember."

"He said he thought you were dead. He was holding you in his arms when you woke... when you came back to life. He told you that he loved you," Gabby said with a sad smile. "Men, huh? Takes a tragedy."

"He—"

"I don't understand it, but vampires seem to feel things a lot deeper than humans do. If he says he loves you, then he really loves you."

Gazing at her hands, she wondered what she was supposed to do. "I can't go outside," she whispered.

"The sun burns. I don't know if I can stomach the thought of living off… blood."

"You're thinking of the cons," Gabby said. "There are some good things."

"Good things? What good things?"

"You're super strong. You're fast. You don't run out of breath. You can jump high. You can see things in high definition. You'll look hot forever…"

"Forever," Liz scoffed. "Immortality. Who'd have thought it, huh? Liz Evans, immortal blood sucker."

"Here," Gabby said, "give me your hand."

Holding out her hand, palm up, Liz wondered what she was doing. The witch dropped a silver ring into her palm. A pretty thing with an onyx stone set into delicate scrollwork.

"What's this for?" she asked, frowning.

"It'll help you with the sunlight. Sam and Zac, they have a web weaved on their bodies. I can't do that, I'm not strong enough, so for now, you get a ring."

"I can go outside? I won't burn?"

"Yep. Just put it on and you're set."

Liz turned the ring over in her hand, inspecting the stone, before slipping it on her right ring finger. "Where did you get it?"

"It was Sam's. I think he said it belonged to his

mother at some point. It was all we had. I spelled it, but I think we should test it first."

Sam's mother's ring? How could she accept such a gift?

Gabby's expression fell. "You still have to complete the change, Liz. Sam says you're still transitioning, so you'll feel sick until you choose."

Truthfully, Liz didn't want to die. She didn't really want to be a vampire either, but Sam had learned to control it. He was practically human in everything he did, despite his dietary requirements. He'd help her. He said he loved her and a feeling in her heart said she did, too. How could she turn her back on that? How could she turn her back on her family?

"Oh my God," she gasped. "What about my mom and dad?"

"That's a hurdle we'll jump when we get there." Gabby took her hand and gave it a squeeze. "Together."

Liz glanced up at her friend and a tear slid down her cheek. "Gabby... I don't want to die."

CHAPTER 5

Liz looked into Sam's eyes and didn't quite understand what she was feeling... or seeing for that matter. The world was sharper in more ways than one. That thing that'd been blossoming between them seemed deeper than it should be after only three weeks.

"Are you sure you want to do this?" Sam asked, sitting on the bed next to her.

She nodded slowly, hugging her arms around her stomach. "I don't want to die, but I don't want to be something I don't understand. What choice do I have? The one that sucks the least."

Zac stood in the doorway, leaning his broad shoulders against the doorframe, arms crossed. He was frowning, gaze cast to the floor. Gabby sat on the opposite side of the bed, looking sick.

"Okay," Sam said.

"What do I need to do?"

"You need human blood to complete the change."

"Will it hurt?" she asked, her gaze flickering to Zac as he let out a snort.

"Yes, it'll hurt," Sam replied.

She saw the knife in Gabby's hand and watched as her friend sliced across her palm, opening a long wound that immediately began to bleed. Holding her hand out, she nodded. "Take it."

A ravenous hunger overtook her, and Liz almost pounced on Gabby in her need for the thing that would save her life. The copper tang hit her tongue and it was enough to cause a reaction in her changing body. She just wasn't expecting it to be as violent as it was. She doubled over with a cry as the blood made its way into her stomach, leaving a burning trail that began to spread through her veins.

Sam slid onto the bed behind her, rubbing her back. "We're not going anywhere."

Her gaze collided with Zac's as another spasm tore through her. She'd never seen anything but smug arrogance from the elder of the brothers, but now she saw pity.

Was it, though?

Before she could contemplate it anymore, her

heart sliced in two and he looked away with a grimace. A split-second later, he was gone.

"Don't fight it, Liz," Sam murmured, holding her close. "Let it take you and it will be over before you know it."

How could she give in? It was her natural impulse to fight.

"Listen to him, Liz," Gabby said from someplace far away.

Collapsing back into Sam, she took a deep breath and let it out slowly. The funny thing was, she didn't need to take another.

There was only one word she could think of to describe how turning into a vampire felt.

Agony.

Zac sat in the parlour, a bottle of whisky in his hands, trying not to listen to the pain that Liz was going through.

It was a pain he was all too familiar with. He'd gone through it and it was his fault Sam had endured it, too. Watching his little brother turn was enough torture to last a lifetime. Scratch that, it was enough torture to last his immortality.

Liz had been attacked in the forest by

werewolves who were lured out of the bayou. Someone had come along between the attack and the time Sam had arrived and fed her vampire blood. Was it an attempt to save her? Then why had they left her alone to die, or worse, turn on her own?

Taking a long draught of alcohol, he felt the slow burn of hunger dissipate in the back of his throat. Sam loved her—he knew it beyond a shadow of a doubt. He was a little jealous, but who knew how these things worked? Sam would take care of her in his spineless absence.

He listened as silence descended on the manor. She'd probably passed out from the pain, her human body giving way to the vampirism that was taking over. She wouldn't feel any pain now.

He heard footsteps on the stairs and a moment later, Gabby glanced at him as she passed the door to the parlour. She gave him a small smile—*so hell had definitely frozen over.* He listened to her rustling around in the kitchen as Sam came into the room, looking beaten.

"How is she?" he asked, dropping his asshole façade.

"Scared." It was frightening how drawn and worried his little brother looked. Sam was usually the one in complete control.

"She'll be okay. It'll pass." He offered the bottle

of whisky to his little brother, who took it and downed a quarter of the bottle.

"She doesn't remember what happened."

"None of it?" Zac asked as Sam sat next to him.

"She remembers running, then nothing until she woke up here."

"It's no wonder, little brother. The way you said you found her, she's lucky she can't remember."

Sam scowled at him. "There's nothing lucky about it."

"It could be worse. I remember everything. Waking up on top of a pile of corpses, choking on my own blood."

"Zac—"

He held up a hand to stop him from saying anything else. "Don't."

Turning away, Sam ran a hand over his face. "She smelt like werewolves—"

"She still smells like them," Zac interrupted. "It's not your fault, Sam."

"I should've known our return would've stirred up something. The South is full of them."

"It's not your fault." If it was something Zac knew about, it was blame and his little brother had nothing to do with this. "Whoever turned her could still be hanging around. I'm going to search the forest, the town, everywhere. Stay here with her.

She'll be confused when she wakes. Turning is hard enough without waking up alone."

Sam nodded. "Do what you have to do."

Zac didn't have to ask twice what he meant. Venturing out into the lengthening afternoon, he let his senses fly out as far as he could manage.

They'd vetted the town carefully before setting up residence. There were no known supernaturals within a fifty-mile radius. Not even a whiff of wet dog or the stench of other vampires. Their legacy had obviously had a long effect on the area, and it kept a lot more than nosey humans away from the manor. Why the hell were they coming back now?

The werewolves he could understand, it was their natural behaviour to migrate towards vampires. Had the pack from the deep bayou found Liz in the forest and attacked her for sport? It still didn't explain the vampire blood, though.

Had the unknown vampire tried to save her... or simply turn her? Whatever the reason, it was important Zac found them before their scent was lost. Changing a dying girl in the middle of the forest and leaving her to complete it on her own... He was callous, but not a complete, utter maniac. Who the hell would do something like that?

Time was running out if he had any hope of picking up a trail from the wolves or the unknown vampire—a vampire that obviously had no issues with the sun.

Setting out across the yard, he focused on the task at hand, because if he focused on what had just happened at the manor...? That was a rage no one wanted to be on the receiving end of.

Liz sat on the crumbling stone fence that separated the overgrown garden beside the Degaud manor from the driveway at the front and stared up at the sky with new eyes.

There were more stars than she could ever hope to count and more than she'd ever seen with her human eyes. They sparkled overhead with silver light, planets, galaxies, satellites... She imagined she could see them all.

When she'd woken up, it was just as Sam had said. She didn't feel any more pain. Instead, she was bombarded with new sensations. Sight, smell, sound, strength, speed. Everything was dialled up to a billion. She'd opened the door and almost pulled it off the hinges, and when she'd turned on the faucet in the shower, it almost came off the wall entirely.

She just needed a little quiet, so she'd retreated

out into the yard in the darkness, but even here, there was a whole new cacophony of sound.

When she felt Zac before she saw him coming, she didn't quite understand how, but she wasn't surprised. He approached her from the garden, picking his way through the overgrown plants, prowling like some kind of wildcat.

He jumped up on top of the wall, higher than any human was able, not bothering to hide what he was anymore. He settled next to her without a word and she could smell the bayou on his skin. He'd been out looking for her attackers and her twisted saviour.

"Did you find anything?" she asked after a moment.

He sighed, betraying how exhausted he felt. "No."

"You didn't stay."

He said nothing, he just pulled out a silver flask and unscrewed the cap.

"Well?" she asked, beginning to get annoyed at his silent treatment.

"No, I didn't stay."

She wanted to slap him for leaving her, but how could she be angry with him? They hardly knew one another, not like her and Sam.

"It's going to be hard, Liz," he said, turning the

flask over and over in his hands. "I can't lie to you. You'll want to eat everyone for a while."

She paled. "How long?"

He shrugged. "I don't know."

"How long did it take you?"

Grimacing, Zac said, "It took Sam a few weeks. He was always good with people."

"I didn't ask about Sam," she snapped.

"Easy, beautiful."

"Answer the question, Zac."

Taking a deep breath, he said, "I've still got issues with it."

Would she be like that? Always struggling with her desire for blood? She felt it now, burning in her throat, aching through her veins.

"I know I'm an asshole. I get it," he said, distracting her from her thoughts.

"That it's easier to have people hate you than let them get close?" Liz asked, narrowing her eyes at the flask in his hand.

He tensed so slightly that she almost missed it.

"That's why, isn't it?" she prodded.

"No," he said through gritted teeth. "It's because I'm a monster."

Her skin prickled. Wasn't she the same now? "Then why are you helping me? Why do you care?"

Zac looked away, biting his bottom lip. "Because you don't deserve it."

"Did you?"

"Hell, Liz."

"Did you have to threaten Gabby's family? Or was that just to prove how big and bad you are to the world?"

"Well, I can see you're going to love being a vampire," he said, rolling his eyes.

"What's that supposed to mean?"

"Emotion overload, twenty-four-seven. You're on a bender right now."

"You need to apologise to Gabby."

Rolling his eyes yet again, he said, "Fine, I'll apologise."

"You so aren't."

"Nope, but I feel sorry, so it counts in my world."

They sat in the darkness on top of the crumbling brick wall, both unsure as to what to say next. Zac would probably always be biting back, getting in the last word.

When he finally said something, she wasn't expecting regret. "If we hadn't come back..."

"It's not your fault," she said.

Why did he have to take the blame for everything? What was so bad in his past that he kept kicking himself down all the time? Zac cared for her in his own way, she saw it now, but she'd always want Sam.

"You don't have to take the blame for everything," she whispered, knowing that he'd hear.

His fingers tightened around the flask and he took another mouthful before handing it to her.

"Why do you drink so much?" she asked, sniffing at the opening. Scotch seemed like it was Zac's drink of choice.

"It helps with the cravings."

"Cravings?"

"Blood. When you get hungry, your throat burns. Alcohol helps."

"How much do you have to drink to get drunk?"

"A great deal more than you used to, that's for sure."

She pressed the flask to her lips and grimaced as the liquor burned a trail right into her empty stomach.

Zac glanced at her out of the corner of his eye, watching her expression. "You'll get used to it."

"I don't think I'll ever get used to it," she said, shaking her head.

"You've got the time."

She snorted at the irony. *Time*. She guessed she had enough of it now to figure out what she was meant to do with her life. Her very long life.

"We'll be here to help you, Liz. We won't let you deal with this alone."

"Good, because I have no idea how to get through another day without you."

Zac looked her up and down with an expression she didn't understand, and she wondered if she'd said the wrong thing.

"It'll be okay," he said. "It has to be."

Liz stood on the sidewalk outside the tiny door next to the hardware store that led up to her apartment. Living above a shop didn't sound like the ideal place to be, but it was her own space and it worked for her. Now it just seemed too noisy.

Gabby had called Mrs. Greene for her the day after she'd died and weaved a story about Liz being sick. It'd bought her a week, but it was time she went home and began to face the inevitable. Life went on, so there was no use hiding from it.

"But you said I have to be invited in," she said to Sam, looking at the door with a frown. "I rent it out, surely I need to be invited by the landlord?"

"Loophole," Sam said.

She gave him a look.

"Hey, I didn't write the rules," he said with a

chuckle. "The mystical part of the universe did. You signed the lease, so technically, it's your home."

Opening the door, she picked up the wad of mail that'd been delivered in her absence. It didn't escape her notice that one was a little larger and thicker than the rest and her heart skipped a beat.

Sam's hand slid over the small of her back and she sighed. She'd forgotten that he could hear those kinds of things.

Handing her keys to Sam, she nodded up the stairs to her front door at the top. "If you think we can get in, you go first."

Threading his fingers through hers, he tugged her up the stairs behind him. Unlocking the door, he stepped inside. "See. Told you."

With a relieved sigh, Liz followed and closed the door behind her. At least she could get into her apartment, that was a good start. Good things were thinner on the ground over the past week, so that was a win she was taking straight to the bank.

Dumping all the letters but one onto the kitchen counter, she held the biggest one in her hands, the emblem of UCLA in the top corner. What was she supposed to do now? Open it probably, but everything was different now.

"Is that...?" Sam asked, looking over her shoulder.

Ignoring him, she stared down at the package and ripped it open with trembling fingers. Forgetting she was stronger now, she nearly tore the entire thing in half.

Reading the cover letter, she already knew what it said before she read the word 'congratulations'. She'd gotten in. She'd gotten into UCLA.

It seems like some kind of cruel joke, she scoffed to herself. *A vampire going to college.*

"Liz?"

She looked up at Sam and handed him the letter. "I can't go now, can I?" She felt tears threatening and wondered if that was just her stupid vampire feelings overloading again.

"You can always put it off for a year," he said. "Get a handle on things first."

"I've been waiting for this for what seems like forever."

"You can still go, Liz. You can still live as much of a normal life as anyone."

"Normal?" She wanted to yell at him to stop being so blind. "I won't age. I can't stay anywhere longer than a few years because people will start to notice. I can't make any human friends because I may eat them. I'll always have to control myself in more ways than I can count. I'll always have to hide. How is that *normal*?"

Sam ignored her protests and pulled her against his chest, winding his arms around her.

"What a screwed-up love story." She sighed into the crook of his neck, taking comfort in the whoosh of his blood she hadn't noticed before.

"Love story?" he asked, resting his cheek against the top of her head.

"I don't believe in insta-love."

"I do," he told her.

"Good for you."

They just stood there, in the middle of her apartment, tangled in each other for what seemed like an hour before she worked up the courage to tell him what Gabby had told her before she'd decided to change. "I know what you said."

"What did I say?" he asked.

"In the forest."

"I thought you didn't remember."

"I don't. Gabby told me. I asked her and she told me."

"Why didn't you say anything?"

She shrugged, not game enough to look him in the eye.

"It's okay," he murmured into her hair. "It's been a tough week."

"You can say that again."

"You don't have to make a decision about college

right now. You've got a bit of time before you can accept or defer, right?"

A year. An entire year to get a grip and find out who she was all over again. Ironically, she didn't have a choice anymore. She was a vampire and would always have to compensate.

She was a vampire and there was no going back.

"Sam?" she asked, her voice a mere whisper.

"Yeah?"

"I think I could love you."

"Well, I know I love you."

He pushed her back, cupping her face, and their eyes met. She didn't have to ask if he meant it, it was all there for her to see. Vampires were weird in an emotionally charged kinda way.

"I'm going to look after you, Liz Evans," he murmured. "Whatever it takes."

Then he kissed her, and she wanted to believe him so much. She had to believe him because there was nowhere else to go.

She'd be okay as long as Sam Degaud was by her side.

PART II

A YEAR AND A BIT LATER...

CHAPTER 6

Afternoon sunlight streamed through the curtains, dappling over Liz's outstretched legs. It was eighteen months after the day Sam found her in the forest and things seemed as well as they could be. She had a handle on the whole vampire thing, and it didn't seem like that much of an inconvenience anymore. With everyone's help, she'd found the perfect balance between human and immortal bloodsucker.

Time was pressing on and she'd deferred her college placement another six months. There wouldn't be another chance, so she had to make a decision like yesterday. She'd thought that after battling two-thousand-year-old vampires and witches that she'd have life worked out at least a little, but Liz couldn't fathom any of it anymore. Her little world had exploded into blood feuds, unrequited love, ancient curses... all kinds of crazy stuff. College seemed to pale in comparison to all the things her friends were going through.

At least she didn't want to eat anyone anymore. There was always that.

Sam sat next to her on the sofa in her apartment, looking utterly beaten. Zac had disappeared with a broken heart, which was bad enough on its own, but he'd left with Regulus, the two-thousand-year-old founding vampire and he was one hundred percent bad guy.

How many founders was that now? Caius was the first, then Arturius—both dead. Regulus was the last who still drew breath, thanks to Aya. Aya, the Witch Hunter, who'd broken Zac's heart beyond repair. What else had she done that was good for them? *Nothing*.

"Aya came to see me at the café today," she said, squinting in the sunshine.

"Really?" Sam asked, snapping out of his thoughts.

"I'm not stupid, Sam. I have a bad feeling she compelled me. I know she can do it."

"What makes you say that?"

"She was in and out in ten seconds flat. She's

never wanted to speak to me voluntarily before. I know Aya has done a lot for us, for Zac, but it's too coincidental, especially after what she did to him." Teach Zac that he was able to love all along, then rip out his heart.

"I think it's better to be in the dark where she's concerned."

Sam's expression changed so quickly, she was sure he knew more than he was letting on. Something told her not to press the matter, so she didn't.

They sat for a while, their legs pressed together. Zac had only left that morning and already Ashburton seemed empty without him. She kind of missed his arrogant comebacks.

"Do you think he'll come back?" she asked. Gazing at Sam, she took in his features. He was worried about his brother, which wasn't anything new, but it seemed almost painful this time.

"Zac's always struggled with his vampire side," Sam replied. "He's gone off like this before. Sometimes for five or six years, sometimes ten or more. This time, I don't know. He really loves Aya. The consuming kind of love." He glanced over and took her in, cupping her face in his hand. "It could either destroy him or save him."

"How could you just let him go like that? Why don't we go after him?"

"I want to. I've wanted to every single time, but I know he needs to do this on his own. Zac's either going to come back a better man or we'll never see him again. Dead or alive."

"I just—"

"I know. I want to help him too, but he doesn't want it."

She supposed that was it. After everything, she had a better handle on the whole vampire thing and it didn't seem such a burden anymore. Maybe it was time to think about what was next and put her dreams first again. Sam was right, she couldn't help Zac.

"Have you given any thought to UCLA?" Sam asked.

Thankful for the change of topic, she nestled against his side. "Yeah, actually... I need to let them know by the end of the week or my place is gone."

"It's the perfect time to go, Liz. No more founding vampires or crazy witches to interrupt anymore."

"What about you? I can't leave you on your own, Sam. Not after Zac—"

He pressed his fingers over her lips. "I'll come, too."

Liz tilted her head to the side, asking him a silent question.

"I've been on my own before," he explained. "It's not like I can't handle it, but wherever you are, so am I." He pressed a quick kiss on her lips.

"College?" she asked with a small grin. "You and thousands of humans aged eighteen to twenty-five out looking for a party?"

"I'm sure there's a great deal of them not looking to get drunk at frat parties every weekend."

"You'd really come?"

"Of course. I told you. You're stuck with me."

"Vampires in the sun." She laughed at the irony.

"Vampires at the beach."

"Now there's a thought."

Turning her thoughts into UCLA, she felt a burst of hope for the first time in months. Maybe now she could live that normal life that Sam had told her was possible. Well, as normal as she could get.

There was no reason why she couldn't do the things she'd always wanted to. They just had to approach them from a different angle.

Things were finally looking refreshingly normal.

Friday nights hadn't been the same since Aya had come to town. If Liz wanted to get technical about it, they hadn't been the same since Alistair had shown up looking for Aya.

Alistair was the vampire who'd been in league with Victoria—the woman who'd changed the brothers all that time ago. It was a twisted story, but Alistair hadn't planned to find Zac the day he walked into *Max's*. Revenge on the elder Degaud brother for killing his lover was last on his list, but he took it, nonetheless. Zac had killed him, but that's when their real trouble had begun.

After that, it'd been all about ancient witches, founding vampires, and witch hunters, so Friday nights at *Max's* had fallen by the wayside in favour of battling evil.

Liz let out a long sigh, staring off into nothing. It was their first Friday since Zac had left and it just didn't feel right anymore.

"You okay?" Gabby asked, bringing her back to reality. They sat in their usual booth at the back, a sort of reclaiming, with drinks and a basket of fries between them. Just like old times.

"Yeah. I'm just thinking about the past few months." She curled her fingers around her glass of scotch—an unconscious ode to Zac maybe—and sighed again.

"Is Sam coming?"

"He's off with Alex picking up his new truck."

"Oh yeah. They finally got around to that?"

When Arturius had kidnapped Gabby a few months back, he'd totalled Alex's truck in the process. That was a messed-up day to say the least. Alex had been shot in the stomach and it was the first time Liz had used her blood to heal someone. Then Gabby had hit the founding vampire with Alex's truck and that was the end of that. After it was all over, Sam had promised to replace it.

"It was just delivered to the dealership. I can't believe Sam bought him a brand-new one."

"Where can I get a rich boyfriend?" Gabby asked.

"I think I lucked out on that one."

"So, isn't your deadline this week for UCLA?"

Liz nodded. "Friday."

"Have you made a decision?"

"I'm going." She smiled at the grin that was on her friend's face. "I mean, it sucks about Zac and everything, but Sam says he'll be okay. I've gotta do something for myself. I can't keep holding back to help people who can't be helped."

"I don't think it's a matter of not being able to help him," Gabby said, her smile fading. "I think he just doesn't want it. Being able to get through things on his own is a big thing with Zac."

"I still worry about him. Especially since he's gone with Regulus."

Gabby cast her gaze down, playing with her napkin. It didn't escape Liz when the witch's heartbeat changed, and she wondered if Gabby knew more than she was letting on.

"Do you know something?" she asked.

"No."

"*Gabby*."

"Just let it go, Liz." She drew in a sharp breath, signalling she wasn't into talking about it.

"Did Regulus do something to you?"

"Liz, it's over. It doesn't matter. I dealt with it and it's fine."

She didn't like the look on her friend's face, but something told her to drop it. Nodding, she sat back in the booth and took a sip of her scotch to soothe her throat.

"I'm going to Europe," Gabby declared abruptly. "It's time I got out of this stink hole since everyone else is."

"Gabby," Liz exclaimed, beaming from ear to ear.

"I've always wanted to go, and after all the crap we've been through... I'm so gone."

"When?"

"Tomorrow."

"Tomorrow?" she almost shrieked. "That's so soon!"

"If I don't go now, I'll never get there." Gabby shrugged. Pointing to Liz's ring, she said, "I can fix that, you know. Spell your body if you want. God knows I'm strong enough now."

Smiling, Liz nodded. Her friend had come such a long way in the past year and a half. She'd found her estranged grandmother Sophia, awakened her power, and battled all the crazy beside her friend and then some. Gabby had turned into a badass witch she was proud to call friend.

"It would be good not to have to rely on a ring to stop me frying to a crisp," Liz said. It'd once belonged to Sam's mother back in the 1860s and she'd never think of taking it off, but it would be nice to have a backup... just in case. Gabby had spelled it the day Sam had found her dying in the forest. It meant a lot, knowing where it came from.

"Let's do it before we go home later, okay?"

"Deal."

Gabby sighed. "I can't believe you're going to college. In L.A. of all places."

"I can't believe your ditching Ashburton and going to Europe. I'm so jealous."

"You've got a rich boyfriend," Gabby said with a laugh. "He can take you over semester break."

"I'm going to miss you, Gabby. Like you wouldn't believe."

"Me, too."

"All our dreams are finally coming true."

Gabby's smile faded and when she replied, Liz wasn't quite sure if she meant a word she said, "Yeah... I guess they are."

CHAPTER 7

L.A. was a world apart from Ashburton. It was just as hot, but it was a different kind of heat. Instead of humidity from the swamp, the air was full of the dry radiance of the desert.

Sam had found them a prefect little apartment close to the UCLA campus. Liz was beyond thankful for the luxury—it made for one less complication having to hide all her weird vampire tendencies from a roommate, especially the invitation part.

In the few weeks before classes officially started, they spent them getting to know the city. They went to the beach, wandered the city, went out to eat, and went dancing. Sam even took her to Disneyland. She descended into fits of laughter every time she pictured him riding the teacups with her. The photo they'd taken with Cinderella was currently pinned to the refrigerator, much to his disgust.

Liz didn't know if she could love him more than she did right now. Everything was working out just as he said it would. Their lives had become as normal as they could get and they didn't have a worry in the world, apart from Zac's lingering absence.

She stood in the middle of the lounge room in their little apartment, unpacking the stack of books she'd just purchased from the campus bookstore. The entire campus was alive with students new and old—so much so, that it took her nearly two hours to get through the line for her class schedule, then another hour at the bookstore.

The front door opened and she glanced up at Sam, who strode in with his own pile of books.

"What's that?" she asked with a frown. He was up to something.

Dumping his books on the sofa, he waved his class schedule at her and winked.

Her mouth fell open. "What did you do, Sam Degaud?"

"Enrolled." He shrugged like it was no big deal.

"But—"

"I can do this thing with my eyes..." he trailed off, a wicked grin on his face.

Her eyebrows rose. "You compelled your way into college?"

"Well, when you say it like that..."

She slapped him across the arm with her copy of Jane Austen's *Persuasion* she needed to read for her Lit class. "If I knew it was that easy, I would've skipped all the essays."

"Seriously, how many vampires want to go to college?"

"Um, two that I know of." Sam pulled her close and planted a kiss on her forehead. "What are you majoring in? Do you know?"

"Business," he replied. "I figured I didn't get to finish it the first time around, so..."

She knew enough about his past to understand he'd been visiting his family during a semester break when his entire life had changed. He'd gone away to study at some ancient fancy college after Zac had run off to join the Confederates. He'd been the one left to take over the family legacy in his brother's absence. Zac had supposedly died in the Civil War some time later and Sam had gone home to be with his family the first moment he could. Little did they know, Zac was a different kind of alive.

"So, do we have any classes together?" she asked, steering the conversation to safer waters.

"One." He flopped down next to her on the sofa.

"And what one's that?"

"Biology," he said with a chuckle before capturing her in a kiss.

"I don't take biology."

"It's a class of two."

———

Liz managed to find her first class without much trouble.

The first one was always the hardest and now that she'd 'broken the seal,' she hoped it'd be a little easier from then on.

Walking into the classroom, she saw it was one of those enormous lecture halls with tiered seating and a large whiteboard and projector screen at the front.

Picking a spot right in the middle, she sat and put her bag between her feet, then pulled out a notebook and pen. Watching as other students continued to pour into the room, she suddenly felt tiny for an immortal vampire. Who'd have thought *Introduction to English Literature* would be so popular? There had to be seats for at least two hundred people, and they were filling up quickly.

A girl sat in the seat next to her and she offered a friendly smile, but the girl glared and looked away.

Okay, then. Rolling her eyes, she glanced away. Big city mentality was obviously worlds apart from the small-town pleasantries she was used to.

A guy was standing in the row directly in front and when she looked up, he offered her a small smile. Obviously, he'd seen the exchange and she wasn't going for a repeat performance, so she smiled a little less broadly, then glanced back at her notebook. College was supposed to be the adventure of a lifetime, right? That's what everyone said it was. She didn't have to make friends day one, she just had to get through an entire day without getting lost... or found out.

Anyway, *could* she make friends? Maybe getting too close was a bad idea.

Calm down, Liz, she thought. *Just get through one day at a time. Save the existentialism for Psych 101.*

Like a cliché, the professor was a balding, middle-aged man in a tweed jacket. As he scrawled his name and the class schedule on the whiteboard, the now-packed room quieted down. Her gaze ran over the guy in front of her, the one who had smiled at her, and felt a weird sensation on the air. Something *tingled* and she wondered if her vampire side was trying to tell her something.

He had curly blond hair, darker at the roots, so

maybe it'd been bleached lighter by the sun. But his skin was pale and had no sign of a tan at all. Maybe he'd moved here from a colder climate? She focused her hearing on his heartbeat, but it was regular, so was his breathing, but as if that'd tell her anything. Pretending to sniff to cover her tracks, all she could smell from the guy was cheap cologne.

As the professor rattled off the course syllabus and assignments for the semester, she couldn't take her eyes off the guy. Staring at the back of his head, she couldn't pinpoint it. Somehow, he seemed familiar, but she was positive she hadn't seen him before. Remembering when Aya had first shown up in Ashburton, she'd felt the same vibration in the air. Was this guy a vampire? If he was, then what was he doing in a college literature class? God, what the hell was *she* doing here?

Before Liz knew it, the class was over and she hadn't heard a thing. She'd been that obsessed with figuring out the guy in front and when he actually turned around and caught her staring, she glanced away quickly, thankful that she didn't blush.

"Are you as lost as I am?" the guy asked, leaning over the back of his seat.

Liz looked him up and down and decided there was no harm in talking to him. Maybe it would settle her misgivings. "Glad I'm not the only one."

He smiled up at her. "I'm Will, by the way."

"Liz."

"Wanna check out the coffeehouse?" he asked. "I don't have another class for a few hours. We can compare notes. I think I'm going to need all the help I can get."

She held up her blank notebook. "I didn't take any."

"Shit, well, all the more reason we need each other."

If the guy was a vampire, what harm could he do in a public place? "Okay," she said. "My next class isn't until two, anyway."

"I totally sense I'm being used to fill up time," Will said with a wink, "but I'll take it."

"Did you move here?" she asked as they walked across campus.

"Yeah. Florida."

"Wow, that's a long way. Why L.A.?"

"Long story." He shrugged and looked away, obviously uncomfortable with her question.

His caginess sent alarm bells ringing, but maybe it was just because of all the crazy she'd been through in the past few months—it'd make any sane person overcompensate. Maybe Will didn't want to speak about it because he genuinely didn't want to for normal reasons—family troubles, broken heart... that kind of normal.

"What about you?" he asked.

"Generic small town, Louisiana."

"Big city living, huh?"

"Something like that."

It wasn't until they stood in front of one of the coffee shops, that she realised they'd walked all the way from the lecture hall in easy conversation. She'd always been good at making friends, but that was in Ashburton when she was human, and this was the big time and she was a vampire with too many secrets to keep. Still, she wondered what Sam was doing.

"What's your poison?" Will asked as they joined the line for the cashier. "My treat."

"It's fine, I can get my own." She made a mental note to mention her boyfriend at some stage.

"Seriously. Consider it a one-off welcoming gift."

"Okay, well, just a standard, classic cappuccino." Glancing around, she saw how busy it was. Students sure loved their caffeine fixes. "I'll grab us a seat."

Finding two free chairs in the middle of the fray, she watched Will wait in line. She scrutinised his every movement as he ordered and waited for their coffees to be made. Every step he took was graceful and super coordinated. Was it because he played sports or because he had the heightened reflexes of a vampire?

She thought about the vampires she knew. She'd become so familiar with Zac and Sam that she couldn't tell the difference between human and vampire anymore. Arturius was different again, but he'd been a two-thousand-year-old founder. She'd never met Caius or Regulus, but wouldn't they be the same?

Remembering the night they'd gone to save Gabby from the basement of that house, the night Arturius had taken Aya and Zac, standing out in the back garden, standing over her unconscious friend... she knew if she had to fight, she could do it now. She'd killed two vampires then and what that meant for her, she didn't know, but if she was threatened...

Will placed a takeout cup in front of her and she smiled. Yeah, she could defend herself if it came down to that.

"What are you thinking about?" he asked, sitting across from her.

She shrugged. "Nothing." *Obsessing.*

"You were someplace far away then."

"I'm just thinking about my major. Mainly, the lack of one."

"You just started," he said. "Give it some time."

"What's yours?"

"I'm doing engineering mostly," he replied. "I need an arts to balance out my transcript and literature seemed—"

"Easy?" she prodded.

Will laughed at being caught out and ran a hand through his hair. "Yeah, but I'm not so sure about it now. Do you have any ideas about yours?"

"Not yet. I'm taking it slow first semester."

"No harm in that. I've got a buddy who has been here for two years and still doesn't have one."

It was then she decided to take a risk. If he was what she thought he was, then he would hear a word whispered lower than a human could hope to register. A word that would cause him to look up in panic or something else. It seemed silly, but she didn't know what else to do.

So, she muttered something that would cause him to panic and falter. Raising her coffee, she went to take a sip, instead she said, "I know what you are."

He was looking down at the table, reaching for his cup, but she saw it. His movement stalled so slightly, it was almost not there at all.

"What's your next class?" he asked, not even skipping a beat.

"Psych." *Damn.* She'd need more proof.

The more she thought about it, the more she believed there was something not quite human about him. There was a gracefulness in his movements that most people didn't have and he seemed to hear things that others couldn't. But those things meant nothing; maybe he was simply nervous about starting at a new school, she knew she was.

When they were trying to figure out if Aya was a vampire, Zac had spiked her food and drink with concentrated garlic and silver. Maybe she could try the same thing, or she could just tell Sam. That was probably a bad idea, considering how cut up he was about Zac's absence. She didn't want him to worry any more than he had to, and it was about time she stood up and took one for the team.

This was one mystery she could solve on her own.

It was only day one and Sam was feeling angry with the whole college thing. He was one hundred and forty-nine years old and everyone else... Yeah, that might be the problem.

It wasn't so much his first few classes. It was trying to deal with people who were a lot less mature than he was. He wasn't the same person he'd been the first time round and he wasn't talking about the obvious.

This college thing was going to grate, but as long as it was what Liz wanted, he was going to be here.

When he saw her up ahead, standing out front of a coffee shop, he came to a halt. A guy stood with her —a tall, handsome kind of clean-cut college kid. They were talking and laughing like old friends and he felt jealousy rise in his chest. Instantly, he prowled forwards, intending to make himself known.

He was still ten paces away when Liz looked up and caught his eye. She smiled, her entire face lighting up and he felt a little better.

"Hey," he said, sliding a hand over her waist.

"Hey."

He glanced at the guy, who was watching the exchange with narrowed eyes. Clearly, she hadn't told him she was taken.

Liz squeezed his hip. "This is Will. We have a literature class together."

"Hey," the guy said, holding out his hand.

Sam stared at it, then glanced at Will, and didn't even bother to shake it.

"Okay," he said with a grimace. "I've got to go or I'll be late. I'll see you later."

Sam felt Liz's gaze burning into the side of his face as he watched Will walk away.

"What was that?" she asked.

"What's his story?" Sam asked, ignoring her question.

"He's from Florida studying engineering."

"And why does he need to be in a literature class?"

"He needs an art—" Liz stopped and slapped his arm. "Seriously? You need to mark your territory now?"

"Did you tell him?"

Her expression fell slightly, and he knew she hadn't.

"Why?" he asked.

"It never came up."

His eyebrows rose and for the first time in his afterlife, he was surprised at the force of his jealousy. Even when Liz had kissed Zac, he hadn't felt this kind of rage.

"Sam," she said with a sigh. "He's just a guy in my literature class, that's all."

"You better tell him that."

Sam glanced the way Will had disappeared and saw him in the distance. The guy was just standing in the middle of the path, staring back at them, not moving, his face expressionless. Sam didn't like the look of this guy at all. Something wasn't right.

He didn't have these kinds of problems when he was on his own before. Then, he'd literally been alone. Zac would be able to cook up a diabolical plan to catch the guy out, but he wasn't around to ask.

No. He didn't like the look of him at all.

CHAPTER 8

The more Liz watched Will, the more she realised she was just being paranoid.

He'd done nothing that led her to believe her suspicions had any truth to them. Actually, she kind of liked him. Her stupid obsession seemed... well, stupid.

She started making friends in her classes and kept her 'special needs' under wraps. She was invited to parties and study groups and all her fears that first day faded away. She really started to like college, and everything was normal for a change— no crazy curses, witch drama, or founding vampire sightings at all.

Every week or so, she'd get an email from Gabby with updates on her European travels. Since it was coming up to Halloween, she said she was in

London, preparing to go to a big costume party in some old, haunted theatre. She was so jealous, but Sam just laughed at her and promised to take her once she'd graduated.

Alex was languishing without them but promised to come visit the moment he could get time off work. His business was growing steadily, and he didn't seem to want to leave it in anybody else's hands but his. That was the thing Liz admired most about her friend; he was hardworking and dedicated beyond belief.

Sitting on the sofa in her and Sam's apartment, she balanced a psych textbook on her knee while trying to type one-handed on her laptop. It was probably one of the hardest classes she had and there were a ton of assignments to work through. It only made her dread the final exam more than she probably ought to.

Her cell dinged, breaking her concentration from her assignment. Picking it up, she smiled when she saw it was Will.

Pre-Halloween party. You in?

She texted back. *Halloween's not until next week.*

Her cell pinged almost immediately. *UCLA tradition. The pre-party sets the tone for the real thing.*

She doubted it was a tradition, but it was a party and she'd been studying pretty hard lately. Why not?

"Sam," she called out.

"Yeah?"

"Will said there's this pre-Halloween party tonight. Wanna go?"

Sam stuck his head out of the kitchen and grimaced. He'd never seemed to get over his territorial jealousy whenever she mentioned him.

"We all know how much you like the guy," she said rolling her eyes. "He's seeing that Gloria girl, you know that."

"I still don't like the look of him."

"He's given me no reason to believe he's anything but my friend, Sam."

"He's into you."

"Seriously?" she cried. "Not a chance."

"I still don't like him. There's something off."

"I thought so too, but—"

"You thought so?" Sam was on the verge of a full-blown rage and she flinched. She'd never seen him so angry at anyone but his brother. "How long has this been going on?"

"Since the first day of class, but Sam—"

"And you never thought to tell me? After all we went through with Aya, Arturius, and Regulus? Shit, Liz."

"He's a friend, Sam," she spat. "A *friend*. Nothing more. Is that what you're so angry about?

That I'm going to run off with him and leave you all alone?" Sam's expression fell and her heart twisted. She'd hit him right where it hurt, and she felt a wave of regret crash into her. No, she wouldn't back down. Will had done nothing wrong. "I'd expect this crap from Zac, but not from you."

"That's a low blow."

Snapping her laptop shut and tossing her textbook aside, she got to her feet and stalked into the bedroom. Wrenching open the closet, she pulled out the nicest top she had and changed into it, not stopping to acknowledge Sam, who was standing in the doorway watching her. Shoving past him, she went into the bathroom and fixed her makeup.

"So, you're going?" he asked, thinly.

"Yeah, Captain Obvious." She rolled her eyes and put on her favourite shade of red lipstick.

"Liz, seriously. C'mon. I'm just looking out for you."

"You're looking out for yourself," she hissed. "I'm not your property."

His jaw trembled like he was trying to hold himself together. Whatever he had to say, she wasn't listening. She wanted to go to a party with her friend. She loved Sam, but he couldn't control everything. He had to let go once in a while.

"I'm coming back, Sam. After all the things we've been through, you can't trust me?"

"I trust you," he said. "I don't trust *him*."

Grabbing her cell, she shoved it into the pocket of her jeans. "I can look after myself."

"Don't go out like this," Sam said.

"Go out like what?"

"Angry."

"Yeah, well, that one's on you," she bit out at him and before he could retort, she slammed the front door in his face.

Still fuming from their stupid argument, Liz strode down the sidewalk, determined to prove Sam wrong.

His jealousy was cute at first, but now it was really starting to annoy her. How many times did she have to say it? Nothing was going on between her and Will. Nothing. What did she have to do? She'd made a mistake that one time with Zac, was she going to pay for it forever? Hell, she really *did* have forever.

Going out to a party wasn't really the answer, but she didn't like being told what to do. She was a big girl. She was a vampire for heaven's sake; she had more than enough strength to help herself.

Will was waiting for her down the street from the party, just as he said he would. He was alone, which surprised her, his hands shoved deep into the pockets of his leather jacket.

"Hey," she called out.

"Hey yourself."

"Where's Gloria?" she asked as she gave him a hug.

"Well, we're going through a bit of a rough patch..."

They walked down the sidewalk towards the sound of music in the distance. "What? Seriously? I thought you guys were solid."

"Um, no. There's kinda someone else..." he trailed off and she frowned, hoping Sam was wrong.

There was a shriek up ahead as they rounded a corner and for a moment, Liz expected a vampire to leap out from the bushes, but it turned out to be a simple shriek of laughter.

The party was in full swing, music blared and students were all over the front lawn, the house was ablaze with light and movement.

Liz's heart dropped. The party was at a frat house, which probably meant there was an annoying barrier she couldn't cross. One, *embarrassing*. Two, it would expose her to a ton of students unless she could wrangle herself an invite. Stupidly, that part hadn't crossed her mind.

"C'mon," she said, changing the subject. "Let's have a few drinks, dance, mingle. It'll distract you from your Gloria problems for one night at least."

The front garden was decked out in Halloween decorations, though nobody was dressed up in costume. There were fake spider webs, pumpkins, and all kinds of creepy things stuck in the lawn.

A handsome guy stopped in front of them and waved a plastic pumpkin shaped bucket of candy at them.

"Candy for the pretty lady?" he asked, holding out the bucket.

Laughing, Liz took a few pieces and tossed some to Will.

"See?" she said, elbowing him. "This is gonna be great."

Walking across the lawn, she saw the front door was propped open and she glanced inside, trying to be easy about it since Will was right behind her. Thankfully, a girl was standing just across the threshold who she recognised from one of her literature classes.

Catching her eye, she called out, "Hey, Francie."

"Hey Liz, c'mon in."

With a bright smile, she stepped over the threshold. *Problem solved.*

"Uh, Liz?"

She turned to see Will standing sheepishly outside where she left him. He kicked his foot at the threshold, and it connected with thin air. Instantly, her expression fell when she realised all her insecurities about him were true. He couldn't come inside because *he hadn't been invited.*

"I know you know what this is," he said like he was taking a chance.

Spinning on her heel, she stalked back outside and jabbed a finger at his chest. "I defended you to my boyfriend," she hissed. "All this time, you were keeping this from me when you knew what I was?"

He squared his jaw. "You kept it from me, too."

"I didn't know, Will. I. Didn't. Know."

"I had to be sure," he went on. "I couldn't just say it."

"Yeah, you could."

"No, if I was right about you and you freaked... I can't compel you. Anyway, if you were human and freaked..." He shrugged. "I don't think I could've handled that."

She started at him and realised he was into her. Of course, she knew. He'd practically told her a million times, but she didn't want to hear it. *Ugh, Sam was right.*

"Will," she murmured. "I'm with Sam."

He smiled, but it didn't reach his eyes. "I know."

She hissed, shaking her head.

"I'm sorry, Liz. We can still be friends, right? We can have a good time." He opened his jacket slightly and she saw he had a blood bag pinned to the lining.

"What's that?" she asked, her eyes widening.

"What does it look like?"

"Why do you need that?"

"These things get pretty wild if you haven't noticed," he said, nodding through the door and towards the kitchen where seven kegs were stacked, waiting to be drunk by hormone-crazed college kids. "It's a just in case, you know?"

Narrowing her eyes, she grasped the arm of a passing student. "Invite him in," she snapped.

The student blinked and shook her head. Glancing at Will, she giggled. "Come on in. Enjoy the party."

Will rose his eyebrows and she shrugged. "You heard the human."

Stepping inside, she made a beeline straight for the kitchen and snatched up a red plastic cup. Filling it to the brim from the open keg, she handed it to Will and got one for herself. She downed it all in one go, and the group of guys standing around the island clapped and cheered, wolf whistling their appreciation.

"I'd tell you to slow down, but you know…" Will said.

"I'd say you only live once, but *you know*."

First pouring herself a refill, she tugged Will into the sitting room where some fast, popular dance song was playing. She'd fought with Sam, Will was a vampire, and all she wanted to do was forget and have some fun for a few hours. *Let loose.*

Holding her cup in the air, she danced around to the music, bumping against other people and against Will. She forgot about all her problems for one second and just enjoyed herself. For that one small slice of time, she could forget she was trying to hide the truth about who she was, forget about her stupid fight with Sam, and forget Will's deception. That was until a group of football jocks decided to have a fight in the middle of the room.

There was a crash as a broad-shouldered guy fell on the coffee table, cracking his head against the corner. There was a few cries of annoyance from the crowd as they jostled them to get out of the way.

Liz halted, staring at the blood that was now gushing from the guy's head.

"Liz," Will said, grabbing her arm. "You okay?"

She shook her head to clear it, the stench of blood thick on the air. "Yeah, I..." She felt her throat constrict and her hand flew to her mouth as her fangs began to stir.

But it smells so good... She took a step forwards, but Will put his hand on her arm.

"Liz?"

She blinked and held her breath.

Will's eyes narrowed and he pulled her towards the back door. "Let's get some air, huh?"

She had no choice but to let him drag her out of the house and into the rear garden.

Cool air hit her skin and the scent died away until all she could smell was the earthy tones of the garden that'd been churned up by dozens and dozens of feet.

Liz had let her control slip for one second and it was almost a disaster. What if she'd changed and gone on a rampage in the middle of a room crammed full of college students?

"I told you these things get crazy," Will said, guiding her down the garden path.

Sitting on a bricked edge of a flowerbed, she said, "I thought I had a handle on it."

He sat next to her. "How old are you?"

"Two years, give or take." Two years sounded like a lot of time now, but in two hundred...? Ugh, her throat still hurt.

"That's all?"

"Why? How old are you?"

Will grimaced in the darkness. "Old."

"Spill."

"A hundred and fourteen."

"*Oh...*"

He chuckled. "Well, I can't say I've had that reaction before."

Swallowing, she tried to get rid of the metallic taste in her mouth but it wouldn't go away. It was driving her mad. "You got that blood bag?"

Will opened his jacket. "You need some?"

She nodded. "Just a little. My throat is killing me."

Unfastening the safety pin, he handed it to her. "You on the human stuff?"

"No, but I can take it."

Will glanced back to the house uneasily. "Liz, I don't think that's such a good idea. If you don't—"

"Just give it here." She snatched the bag from him and ripped the top off. "Just a little, okay?"

She'd survived on a combination of human and animal blood in her first six months before weaning off it completely. A mouthful wouldn't hurt, and she knew she could handle it. It wasn't like being an alcoholic. One taste wouldn't send her off the rails because she hadn't been hooked on it in the first place.

The bag hit her lips and the tang of blood hit her tongue and everything came alive. Every nerve ending in her body sung with intense clarity and as it ran down her throat, she felt an overwhelming need. She wanted *more*. She drew another mouthful and felt Will's hand on her arm.

"I think that's enough, Liz."

She shook his hand away and continued to suck the bag dry.

"Liz."

"*No*," she hissed, rising to her feet.

Where was impulse control now? One drop of human blood spoke to all the things that'd been dulled inside of her. Her hearing was sharper, her sight was crisper, and she felt stronger than she'd ever had. The sensation only grew as the blood circulated through her system.

"Liz?"

Her head snapped up at the sound of Francie's voice. They'd been paired together for an assignment in one of her classes a few weeks back and she'd instantly liked her. She was tall, slim, pretty, with a wild head of curly hair, and constantly had a string of guys following her around. But Liz wasn't seeing any of that. All her brain could process were two things—*human and food*. She was so hungry.

"What's up, girl?" Francie asked. "Some party, huh?"

Liz felt Will's hand on her arm, but nothing could've stopped her. She was high on human blood and beyond reasoning.

Launching herself onto Francie, she went straight for her neck, biting into flesh. Blood burst into her mouth and she groaned at the sweet taste, hardly hearing the screams splitting the night air. Her hand clamped down on her friend's mouth as she held her in place, drinking like there was no end in sight.

Hands pulled at her from someplace far away. "Liz, stop. Let her go, you're killing her."

She didn't listen.

"Liz, *stop*."

She was torn away and a wail came from her throat, but it was the split-second she needed to realise what she'd done.

Dropping Francie, she stumbled back and almost fell into the opposite garden bed. Francie sobbed, curling into a ball like it'd protect her from the monster that'd just attacked her. Her heartbeat was slowing, her skin colour was fading, and her eyes...

"I killed her," Liz sobbed, her hands clawing into her hair. "*I killed her.*"

"Shit, Liz. Calm down," Will pleaded with her, but she was too amped up.

She'd killed a vampire before, but never a human. *Never.*

She was covered in blood. It was all over her hands, clothes, her face, in her hair... and it burned.

Is this what Zac felt like? Is this what he had to deal with every single day? She thought she'd understood but it turned out, she didn't even have an inkling.

Sam hovered at the front door of the frat house, unable to get inside. The party was at rager status and everyone was too drunk to notice him, let alone give him an invitation. Scanning the crowd, he couldn't spot Liz, so he rounded the house to try the yard at the back.

He'd called her cell nonstop since she'd left, and she hadn't picked up once. He had a bad feeling and when he got bad feelings, he was usually right about them. He didn't trust Will for good reason. The guy was secretive and cocky and moving in on his girl.

Time to end this stupid pissing match once and for all.

He hated fighting with Liz. He hated that she'd left angry and upset with him. He hated he was so jealous of Will, but he couldn't let it go.

As he rounded the corner of the house, he smelled it immediately. *Blood*. Human blood, and lots of it.

When his gaze laid on the most horrific sight he'd ever seen, he almost lost it. He stared in shock at Liz, who was standing over the inert body of one of her classmates, her eyes black and blood dripping from her mouth onto her blouse. *Oh, hell...*

"Sam, I didn't mean for her to lose it. I didn't mean—"

"Will?" Sam exclaimed, staring straight at him. He knew it. The guy was a vampire.

"I didn't know. She said she was okay—"

"She doesn't drink human blood," he roared, stalking forwards.

"It wasn't supposed to get out of control. I told her to only take a little at a time."

Sam thrust his fists into the front of Will's shirt. "What kind of idiot are you? She could've killed her!"

Shoving the vampire aside, he was in front of Liz in a flash, no longer concerned about hiding what he was. The human girl was hardly conscious, and Will...? Well, he'd deal with him later.

Cupping her face, he stared into her black eyes. "Come back to me, Liz."

Her entire body shook from the high she was buzzing off, tears streaming down her cheeks, smearing the blood she'd tried to wipe away.

"I-I killed her," she choked out.

He shook his head, holding her close. "No, she's going to be okay, but I've got to help her." He guided Liz to sit on the raised stone border of the flowerbed, hardly aware that Will had disappeared. The asshole had fled at the first sign of trouble like the coward he was.

"Stay there," he murmured. "Don't move, okay?"

Liz nodded slowly, her eyes filling with more tears.

Turning back to the human girl, who was shivering uncontrollably against the garden wall, he grasped both her shoulders. She struggled and cried out, but he held her firm, even as she sobbed.

"What's your name?"

"F-Francie."

"Francie, you're going to stay calm, okay?"

She nodded as his compulsion took hold. Taking his wrist, he bit into his flesh, drawing blood. Wetting his fingers, he rubbed it into Francie's torn neck and her face contorted in pain, but as commanded, she didn't make any sound. Soothing her skin, it healed, the flesh knitting back together. Once it was pink and new again, he drew back and placed his hands on her shoulders.

"Now, you're better okay?" he said.

She nodded again. "It's stopped hurting."

"Good. Now, you're going to go home and get cleaned up. You're going to go to bed and get some sleep. The moment I let go of you, you will forget everything that happened here. You will remember having fun at the party, but you had to go home early because you were feeling sick."

"Okay," Francie said, her gaze locked onto Sam's.

Pulling his hands away, she shook her head once and stared at him for a moment. "Oh, hey. I'm just going home. Have fun at the party, okay?"

Smiling, he replied, "Will do."

Francie stumbled to her feet and started walking off like nothing had happened and a moment later, she rounded the corner of the house and was gone.

Holding his hand out to Liz, she stared at it for the longest time before taking it in her own.

"C'mon," he said. "I'm taking you home."

CHAPTER 9

S am held Liz in his arms while she cried herself to sleep.

The human blood was doing a bang-up job of tearing her insides apart and there was nothing he could do but hold her until she was out for the count. She'd wake up with one hell of a headache, vampire or not.

Her cell had been lighting up all night like a Christmas tree, so the moment she was asleep, Sam picked it up and saw the messages Will had left and his anger simmered again.

He scrolled through them and they were all various shades of cowardly.

Are you okay?

Can I see you? I have to make sure you're okay.

I shouldn't have let you take that blood.

Liz, we have to talk.

He wanted to make sure she was okay? Maybe he shouldn't have run off like a scared child the moment things got tough. He hadn't even managed to say he was sorry.

Squashing down the urge to hurl the cell at the wall, Sam sucked it up and texted him back. Someone had to talk to him, and it wouldn't be Liz. Punching in a message, he sent it before he could think twice.

Meet me at the coffee house in an hour.

It was already seven a.m., so eight didn't seem that much of a stretch, and something said Will wouldn't pass up on the opportunity. When a message came back almost instantaneously, Sam snorted. *Asshole.*

Grabbing his keys, he took one last look at Liz. She was still fast asleep and probably would be until tonight. She'd overloaded every nerve ending in her body and was in the middle of the worst vampire hangover in existence. He'd be back by the time she woke up and it would all be over.

When Sam got to the coffee house, he parked his car out back in the alley. Rounding the front in the shop, it was filling up fast with students that lived on residence. They were all looking worse for wear, having breakfast and coffee after a hard night out partying.

Will sat alone at a table inside by the windows, looking at his watch. Staring at the vampire, Sam knew he had to take a page right out of his big brother's playbook. He'd been witness to a lot of threats and follow-throughs in his time, so this should be easy enough.

Pushing open the door, he stepped inside, the smell of roasted coffee filling his senses. Crossing to where Will sat by the window, he put on his poker face. Cool, calm, and collected.

Will tensed as his gaze landed on him.

"Liz didn't send that message, did she?" he asked. There was nothing friendly about his tone and Sam wondered if this was the real Will talking. No pretences, no performance for Liz's sake...

"You and I need to have a little chat." He clapped a hand on Will's shoulder, digging his fingers into flesh with just enough pressure to cause pain. "Out back."

Will stood, the chair he sat on scraping loudly against the floor, and snarled, "Fine."

Pushing the vampire in front, Sam followed him through the coffee house and out a service door at the rear of the store. Nobody was in sight amongst the crates and dumpsters in the small alleyway, and the moment the door slammed shut, Sam pushed Will from behind.

"What do you want with Liz?"

"We're friends," Will replied, turning to glare. "Nothing more."

Sam inched closer, never taking his gaze off the vampire. "See, there's a problem with that, Will... *I don't believe you.*"

Will shifted from foot to foot, his hands shaking and his pupils dilating. Sam didn't like the looks of this. What else was the guy hiding from them? Compulsive tendencies, manipulation. Insanity?

"I think you need to tell me the truth, Will," he said, staring the vampire down. Time to bluff a little. "It's only a matter of time before I find out all the pieces to your sordid little puzzle, and what do you think I'll do then?"

Will's eyes turned black and he fisted his hands into the front of Sam's shirt. "*You need to get out of my way.*"

Sam curled his hands around the vampire's wrists and squeezed. "You need to leave her alone."

"Or what, Sam? What are you going to do?"

"Whatever it takes." He shoved Will hard, dislodging his grip, and he stumbled back into the wall of the coffee house. "What do you want with Liz? I won't ask you again."

Will laughed, running his hands over his face like he was wiping away a mask. His entire expression twisted into something malicious.

"I found her," Will muttered. "I found her dying."

The blood drained from Sam's face. They never found the vampire who had turned Liz.

"I heard someone coming... *You.*" He jabbed a finger at Sam. "I couldn't stay. I couldn't let you see me. I compelled her to forget and I watched you take her from me."

"I took her from you?"

"I saved her from death. I saved her—"

"You created a vampire and left. You wanna talk about responsibility? What do you think would've happened if I wasn't there to help her? How do you think she would've handled the cravings? The sun?"

"*She was mine!*"

Sam blinked hard, clenching his fists. "What did you just say?"

"She was mine, and *you took her from me*," Will snarled, his eyes beginning to change. "I was the one who saved her from the werewolves that you drew to Ashburton. If it wasn't for you, then she would be mine."

Sam drew in a sharp breath. Had he been

watching her? Stalking her? Conspiring to kidnap her and change her into a vampire against her will? It was the same thing that'd happened to Zac all those years ago. Victoria had watched him from afar and the moment he'd been left for dead, she swooped in and took her prize. What resulted was nothing short of torture. Zac still suffered from the things that woman did to him, which was the reason he'd gone off with Regulus to either find his peace or die. *If Liz had suffered the same fate...* The thought made him sick.

"She is not a possession," Sam roared. "She is free to do as she pleases, and I will not let her go with you. Not after you changed her against her will."

"She was dying. What was I supposed to do? *They were always dying...*"

"What? Have you done this before?"

"I save them and give them a gift," Will went on, ignoring his question. "Don't you see? She was the one who would've stayed with me. Me and her, for eternity."

Suddenly, Sam remembered the story Zac told him all those months ago when Morgan—a woman from his past he'd never told Sam about—appeared out of nowhere. The woman who'd found his brother by a dark road in France during the Second World War and brought him back from the brink of insanity. The woman who'd been saved from death by a vampire named…

Will.

His eyes widened at the realisation. "Morgan…"

"*Morgan…*" Will drawled.

"1940s, London. Did you turn a nurse?"

Will regarded him for a moment.

"Did you know Morgan?"

The vampire shook his head. "She wasn't the one."

"You turned her?"

"I suppose I did. She was dying, much the same way as Liz was, but she wasn't the same. Liz—"

"You cared for her then," Sam interrupted. "You taught her."

"She taught herself. She wasn't the one I was looking for."

"The one what?" As Sam asked, he realised the answer. Just as there were psychopaths in the human world, so were there in the vampire one. It wasn't black and white, not by a long shot.

How many other women had he done this to? How many had suffered and died? How many had been turned and left to fend for themselves? How many innocents had died because of this mentally unstable menace?

Will shuffled forwards, an unhinged gleam in his eyes. "Liz is the one, and I won't let you take her from me again."

"How old are you?" Sam asked, stalling.

"What's it to you?"

"Everything."

The vampire took the bait and gave him the information he wanted. "1900, I was turned. And you?"

"Me? 1865, asshole," he snarled.

Grabbing the vampire around the neck, he hurled him across the alley. There was a bang that sounded like a gunshot as the vampire hit the corrugated iron fence and fell face-first onto the asphalt.

A dog started barking somewhere in the distance, and Sam knew he only had a few minutes to get this done before the cops showed up. As Will tried to get to his feet, he was on top of the vampire. With one fluid motion, Sam snapped the vampire's neck and let his limp body fall back to the ground.

Staring down at the psychopath who almost took the love of his eternity away from him, Sam wondered what kind of mercy he deserved. He could just stake him right now and be done with it because death was the only way this was ending.

Sam shook his head. No, staking him would be too quick. He had something a lot more fitting in mind.

Without breaking stride, Sam hauled the vampire's body out into the lot, managing to avoid anyone seeing, and stuffed him into the trunk of his car.

There was a particularly warm spot in hell for guys like Will.

It was already dark when Sam got back to the apartment and Liz was asleep on the sofa. She'd obviously gotten up sometime during the day, decided to wait for him, and fell asleep in the process.

Perching beside her, he ran a hand over her blonde hair. She was precious to him. He'd do whatever it took to protect her over and over again. No regrets.

She stirred, her eyes cracking open.

"Hey," she whispered.

"Hey."

"I'm sorry."

"I know."

"Where've you been?"

"Sorting out a few things."

She sat up, leaning her cheek against his shoulder. "Sorting out Will, right?"

Sam knew he had to tell her the truth. After everything they'd been through together—here and back in Ashburton—she had the right to know about the circumstances that made her the way she was.

"Liz, he was watching you. That day in the bayou."

She paled. "The day I... He—"

"Turned you," Sam finished for her. "He admitted it to my face."

She stared at him with clear blue eyes, disbelief flooding her pretty features. "But—"

"Do you really want to know more?"

"Yes. Sam, what was going on? What—"

"He thought you were his. Because he turned you, he thought it meant he owned you."

"His... property?" Her fingers curled into the folds of his T-shirt like she had to hold on to something or break the apartment into tiny pieces.

"He'd been watching you," Sam said, his jaw stiff.

"Before, when you were still human. He wanted to make you his, but the werewolves sped up the process. He was pissed with me for taking you from him."

"*I think I'm going to be sick.*"

"He couldn't do anything while Zac and I were with you, and I seriously doubt anything he ever told you was true."

"He was working me?"

Sam nodded. "He almost fooled me, too."

"Do you think he would have..." She paused, gesturing at her chest.

"Staked me?" Sam shrugged. "Probably."

"*No.*"

"That's not all," he added.

Liz moaned softly and pressed her palm against her forehead. "There's more?"

"Will was the one who turned Morgan. He turned her for the same reason. He ditched her because she wasn't 'the one'."

Liz gasped, "*Oh my God.*"

"Liz, some vampires don't adjust as well as others..."

"He was insane, right? Not just regular crazy... special vampire crazy, right?"

He nodded, watching Liz's changing expression. It went through shock, surprise, anger, horror before it settled into something he couldn't understand. It would take her a while to process.

"I checked in on Francie," he said, pulling her to his side.

"Is she okay?"

"She's fine and none the wiser."

Liz covered her face with her hands. "*I can't believe...*"

Sam knew as well as the next vampire how things got to them more than when they were human. Liz's guilt was eating her from the inside out to the point it was crippling her. She was so good and pure, seeing her like this hurt his heart.

"Everything is okay now," he murmured into her hair.

"I could have killed her."

"But you didn't."

"This time," she cried. "What if you're not there one day and—"

"*Shh,*" he crooned. "None of us had complete control from day one, let alone two years later. Don't beat yourself up about it. Francie is fine."

Liz shifted against him, raising her head. "I get it. We're still monsters inside, no matter how human we want to be."

It was a hard truth to swallow, but it was true.

They might look the same, feel the same... but inside? They were different.

"Where's Will now?"

Sam shrugged. "He's not going to hurt you again."

"Sam, what did you do?"

He turned and grasped her shoulders. "Listen to me, Liz. He is not going to hurt you again. I dealt with it. That's all you need to know. Please. don't ask me about it again. *Promise me.*"

He saw the disbelief in her eyes and it broke his heart. She suspected what he'd done. Following through on threats was his brother's specialty, not his. He was meant to be the good brother, but even he knew that sometimes extreme measures were needed to protect the people he loved.

Sam didn't regret it, not for one second.

"Okay," Liz murmured, pressing her hand over his heart. "I promise."

At first, Will didn't understand where he was. As he came to, he stared up at the lightening sky, thousands of starts twinkling above.

It wasn't until he tried to move that he realised he couldn't. Pain splintered through his entire body

—through his hands and feet, through his stomach and knees.

Angling his head up, he saw he was impaled with several wooden stakes. Crucified, skewered like a live voodoo doll. No guesses who'd deigned to give him such special treatment.

He was in the desert somewhere outside of L.A. He could smell the sun and sand on the air, as well as baked earth and animals that prowled the night. He'd been dumped in the desert like a corpse.

Sunrise was close. Trying one hand, he cried out as wood scraped against flesh and bone. It would take him hours to free himself and by the time he healed...

When he got his hands on him, he would tear Sam's head off. He would—

Tendrils of smoke rose from his exposed skin and his eyes widened in shock. No, it couldn't happen. It couldn't. There was a witch's web weaved over his body. *He couldn't burn.*

As the sunrise crept farther and farther over the horizon, the closer he came to his body hitting direct sunlight. He felt hot, too hot.

"No!" He roared his anger to the empty desert, thrashing against his restraints.

Even if he broke free, there was nowhere to go, nowhere to hide from the sun. He was done.

Liz was the one. She was his eternity. After so long searching, after so many failures, he'd found her. Sam Degaud would pay. He would haunt his afterlife with all the hate he could muster. In the afterlife, he would have his revenge.

As the sun finally clawed its way across his bare skin, pain exploded, searing as he burst into flames.

CHAPTER 10

F *our months later...*

"Sam!" Liz exclaimed as he ticked her with a blade of grass.

They were sitting in the middle of the greenest, sunniest patch of grass on the whole UCLA campus, surrounded by books and a semester's worth of notes. Liz was trying to study for her last final—Literature, strangely enough. She'd been oh so lucky to have the very last final scheduled in the whole college due to administrative delays. Most students were already done and packing up for the holidays.

"Literature is your best class," Sam said, tossing the piece of grass aside.

"I still have to study," she scolded him. "I'm not a know-it-all like you."

"Hey."

It'd been four months to the day since everything happened with Will. That night at the Halloween party seemed like an age ago, and everything that'd happened after... that seemed like an even more distant memory. Things were good between them again. More than good, they were unbelievable. He loved her so much.

Shaking his head, Sam stilled, feeling something strange in the air. Glancing up, he cast his gaze around the quadrangle. It didn't take him long to see the shadowy figure leaning against a tree like a cocky son of a bitch. He stuck out like a sore thumb.

Shooting to his feet, Liz's books scattered and she cried out, but he only had eyes for the one person he thought he'd never see again... this decade at least.

Approaching his big brother, a stupid grin spread across his face. As Zac came to meet him, they threw their arms around each other.

"Zac."

"Little brother."

Sam drew back and looked him over. "I didn't know if I'd ever see you again, at least not in this decade. How are you?"

"Better than ever."

"Aya?"

Zac gestured behind him, where the raven-haired hybrid sat on a bench. She raised a hand to give him a little wave and Sam shook his head. *Of course.*

"You guys finally worked it out?" he asked.

"Not without some melodrama." Zac threw an arm around Sam's shoulder as they crossed the lawn towards Liz, who was gaping open-mouthed at them.

"There's always melodrama with you. Where have you been?"

"Brother," Zac said, shaking his head, "have I got a story to tell you."

"You've got a story? Wait until you hear about what Liz and I have been doing..."

The End.

THE UNHALLOWED

Book Five in The Witch Hunter Saga

The King is dead...Long live the King.

Nye Saer is four hundred year old vampire. Bad guy, one time leader of the notorious Six who's trying to turn over a new leaf and grow a heart.

With all six Roman founders dead and gone, it's up to him to bring order back to the London underworld, but there's one problem. They don't fear him as much as they should.

Isobel is the human sister of the newborn founder Alex...and you never want to mess with a founding vampire, no matter how good they claim to be. When she turns up on his doorstep, Nye has to go against everything he is in order to protect her from his enemies. But when strange markings begin to appear all over London, unrest amongst the vampires and his conflicting concern over Isobel will be the least of Nye's problems. He's seen the symbols before and there's only one thing it could mean.

The Unhallowed are back...and they're not happy.

The Unhallowed continues the story begun in the Urban Fantasy series, **The Witch Hunter Saga** — *In a world remade, the London vampires must find their way out of chaos...without losing everything to a bunch of blood-thirsty witches.*

The Unhallowed is OUT NOW!

ABOUT NICOLE

Nicole R. Taylor is an Australian Urban Fantasy author.

She lives in the western suburbs of Melbourne dreaming up nail biting stories featuring sassy witches, duplicitous vampires, hunky shapeshifters, and devious monsters.

She likes chocolate, cat memes, and video games.

When she's not writing, she likes to think of what she's writing next.

Follow Nicole Online:

Website: nicolertaylorwrites.com
Twitter: twitter.com/nicole_noir
Facebook: facebook.com/nrtaylorwrites
Newsletter: nicolertaylorwrites.com/newsletter
Email: nicole.this.is@gmail.com